1997 £6⁹⁵

Joan Riley

Photo by Pierre Tran

Joan Riley was born in St Mary, Jamaica, the youngest of eight children. She now lives in Britain; she received her B.A. from the University of Sussex in 1979 and her M.A. from the University of London in 1984. She works for a drugs advice agency, and teaches black history and culture in her spare time. She is actively involved in the struggle for black people's freedom and, whilst feeling that separatism is divisive and counter-productive, supports 'the idea of women organising within the wider framework of black people's struggle to articulate and fight for their particular needs'. She is also a single parent, 'concerned about the problems faced by others, particularly black women who are lone parents, within a system that openly and systematically discriminates against them'. This is her first published work.

She is currently working on a new novel, *Waiting in the Twilight*, the story of an old woman who comes to Britain from the Caribbean in the late fifties, which continues her concern to depict 'the forgotten or unglamorous section of my people', to show black people as three-dimensional, 'neither all good nor bad but a very real part of thinking, feeling, uncertain humanity'.

JOAN RILEY

The Unbelonging

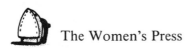 The Women's Press

First published in Great Britain by
The Women's Press Limited 1985
A member of the Namara Group
124 Shoreditch High Street, London, E1 6JE

British Library Cataloguing in Publication Data

Riley, Joan
    The unbelonging
    I. Title
    823'.914[F]   PR6068.I35/

    ISBN 0-7043-2861-5
    ISBN 0-7043-3959-5 Pbk

Typeset by AKM Associates (U.K.) Ltd., London
Printed in Great Britain by Nene Litho,
and bound by Woolnough Bookbinding,
both of Irthlingborough, Northants

For Viola who had the courage to allow a frank
exploration of her life, and for my daughter
Lethna who was a source of constant inspiration
despite herself. And Egbert and Gem the twins,
and Dejenee who lifted my spirit often.

Acknowledgement

I would like to acknowledge the contribution of Beverley Huie who has been ever-patient in spending hours reading and discussing the ideas of the book, and essential in the shaping of it from the original idea to the final draft; Theo Sowa who uncomplainingly read chapters at short notice; Rhonda Cobham who corrected the novel and Ros de Lanerolle who gave tremendous help and support.

Memories

Lianas trailing in sparkling green pools
tempted our childish minds to adventure,
Gullies stretching forbidden and deep
calling us to delve in their mysteries,
Sky blue and smiling beckoning forward
unclouded minds to reach for perfection,
Poised on the edge of unknown worlds
willing to face any challenge they brought,
launching ourselves from that cool
blue and green place,
swinging forever through sun-dappled leaves,
Up, up and higher, higher and higher
maybe to reach to the high wide blue world,
seeing the people, ant specks below us
scurrying madly through myriad adventures,
Unclouded minds saw unclouded visions
then we were young, in a land of our own.

One

The three of them were in their secret place again and the sound of their laughter rose through the sweet-scented bushes from where they lay. Hyacinth felt the lazy warmth of the early afternoon air wrap her in well-being as she lay back in the cool grass, listening idly to the conversation. It was safe in this little green cave, the recesses of the bushes laden with long-stemmed hibiscus and yellow trumpet-flowers and humming with insect activity.

They were talking about the Independence parade just past, and Hyacinth soon lost interest, her mind centred on the warm glow of contentment somewhere in the centre of her chest. She was slipping back, back to the fever of anticipation, the mounting impatience as the minutes on the face of the monument clock slipped slowly by.

Hyacinth was hopping from foot to foot, caught in the excitement, part of that jostling good-natured crowd, craning forward, impatient to see the first float appear. They had been lucky to get a place right at the front, and she pressed closer to Aunt Joyce's reassuring bulk as the crowd surged against her. She was glad of the cane-cutter's hat on her head, and of the little breeze that was so cool where it blew on the wet patches of sweat on her back and under her arms. Aunt Joyce had a big sombrero slung lazily across her bulk, eyes squinting against the glare of the sun, the usual smile on her face as she turned every few minutes to exchange words with her neighbour.

Suddenly there was silence in the crowd. Far away in the distance came the sound of a flute, followed by the boom of a big goatskin drum. Hyacinth's heart skipped a beat, then raced with excitement. She shuffled, as the crowd surged around her, craning forward, pushing out eagerly, wanting to catch her first glimpse of the colourful band float. Her aunt's big hand grabbed her dress, shook her.

'Hyacinth! Hyacinth!'

She shrugged impatiently, trying to shake free of the hand, caught in the excitement of the day. But it gripped on, refused to be dislodged.

'Hyacinth!'

The voice had become insistent, the hand moved to her shoulder, curled round, became biting, vicious, a painful pinch that seemed to pull her back.

'Hyacinth, wake up!'

The voice was no longer the mellow one of her good-natured aunt. Harsh and strident, the accent grated on her ears, as a final vicious shake yanked her away from her peace. Coldness enveloped her, clammy cold fingers dragged her back to consciousness. Her mind struggled in confusion, unable to grasp the change for a few, endless seconds.

'You wet the bed again!'

The words came out on a snap of teeth, a hiss of anger, bringing painful and instant awareness with them. Hyacinth struggled to sit up, eyes opening reluctantly to dingy grey walls, before moving blankly to the equally grey sky she could just glimpse through the ill-fitting curtains.

'Look at me, girl!'

Dull eyes slid sullenly across the mean room, locking apprehensively with protruding bloodshot spite as the yellow-skinned woman glared her hatred down at her.

Hyacinth forced herself to stay calm, not to beg. Her mind still wrestling with the shock of disappointment, she clenched herself against the cold that stung and bit, where the sodden nightdress clung to her in clammy folds. She would have clutched herself for warmth, but knew that the woman would see it as defiance. Instead she hung her head, hands loose beside her on the sheet, becoming gradually aware of feeling slightly breathless, of a pulse drumming in her ears, and her eyes burning with self-pity and the desire to cry.

'Get up, girl,' the woman shouted, as Hyacinth continued to sit in silent misery. She stayed where she was, incapable of response, of obedience, for a few moments. The woman shifted menacingly, and Hyacinth could sense the angry impatience within her. It mobilised her, caused her to push her legs to the floor in an automatic motion. Her whole body was mechanical, twisting jerkily, legs shifting, feet lowered to cold floorboards, dragging her sodden cotton nightdress as she stood. Thin, rank cloth clung to her and the angle of her body was tense and awkward with expectation.

'Wait till your father gets home!'

It was said with triumph, a final blow against an already defeated enemy.

Alone, Hyacinth looked down at the sodden sheet in dismay, shame and fear warring inside her. She could hardly bear to see the extent of the drying yellow stain that marked the outer edges of her disgrace. She had to force her hands not to shake as she pulled the sheet off the bed. The smell of stale urine rose in a wave, disturbed by the movement, and she stepped back in disgust. She would have taken it outside to air across the clothes-line, but fear stopped her. She had done that once before. The sickening crack of rusty guttering parting from the wall remained in her ears. Her body still smarted from the stinging blows of the belt buckle, remembered the ice-cold bath, and the shaking, a mingling of cold and fear, as he had watched her sitting in the water.

Why did it have to be a dream? she thought with sudden savagery. She had been so sure that she was back home, so sure that this time it was the real thing. Christ, she had even pinched herself before settling down with certainty to enjoy her old life. This place, this life had been the dream. Large brown eyes filled with frustrated tears as her mind faltered on the thought, shied away from its meaning. She bit her lip hard, feeling weak at the thought of the evening, the cutting lashes, and the stinging, screaming flesh that would result. It stayed on the edge of her mind all day, just outside her consciousness, waiting for the slightest relaxation to swamp her thoughts with weakening, stomach-churning fear. Every time her mind fixed on a subject, settled down to grapple with it, his face intruded, the smile she hated and feared on his lips. She could imagine how the bulge in his trousers would grow when he heard of what she had done. Time and again she pushed thoughts of him to the back of her mind as the morning lessons wore on, only to have them resurface when she least expected.

Hyacinth had been at Beacon Girls' Secondary School for only two months. Being one of only eight black children, she had become the butt of many jokes, taunts and cruel tricks. Normally the breaks between lessons were the greatest nightmares of the school day, to be approached with apprehension, and then endured when they finally arrived. Today, however, it was not the cruelty of the other children that had her hopping nervously from foot to foot as she stood against a wall in the cold air of the paved playground. Fear was her constant companion, riding her, and as the day wore on, his face became harder and harder to banish; her concentration on the lesson, less and less.

She knew he was home long before she turned the last corner; knew, as she always did, from the large painful blockage in her throat that made it hard to swallow, the sudden heaviness in her legs that seemed to drag her back. It was always like this when she was in trouble. Her hands were clammy by the time she reached the peeling, black gate, but she still managed to register disgust. She hated this house, the way it looked so neglected and ugly between its two well-kept neighbours. The black painted front made it grim and uninviting, something that the gloomy interior did nothing to dispel. No wonder no one ever came to visit them.

Her hands shook as she fumbled to put the key in the lock, and her mouth felt dry by the time the door swung open. There was a sickness in her stomach as she tried to tell herself that he was late, that she had somehow made a mistake, and the bike outside the front gate wasn't his.

'Hyacinth!'

The word was cold, dispelling any hope, a command to be obeyed. She felt her feet stick to the orange, brick-patterned lino in the narrow passage, raised her eyes longingly to the deeper gloom at the top of the stairs.

'Hyacinth! I don't want to call you again.'

Sweat broke out on her forehead, in her palms, prickled under her arms and on her back. She rubbed her palms nervously against the sides of her blue school skirt, not sure she could move, two fears warring, fear of his anger winning, impelling her forward.

He was sitting in his usual chair in the bay window on the opposite side of the room, the smile that had haunted her day on his lips, and she wished illogically that he would turn into Aunt

Joyce with her smooth brown cheeks and twinkling dark eyes. Her eyes slipped round the shabby room as they had done so many times before. She hated it as much as she hated the house, hated the fruit bowl, the wallpaper, the orange sail curtains, the blue chairs and settee, the television, him . . . yes, especially him. But him she must not look at, had to force herself to look away from. She did not dare let her eyes drift down, afraid they would confirm what her frightened mind already knew.

She knew he would keep her standing there until her nerve went; knew he would wait for the tears to slip out, the shaking to start. She could feel her eyes burning, misery and self-pity swamping her, and she fought back the tears determinedly. Her whole being was tensed, ears straining for what she dared not look at. She could imagine him easing forward, lifting the seat cushion, and pulling it out . . .

She wrenched her mind away, feeling a shiver already threatening. She would be brave, would not let him frighten her like this, would think of something pleasant. Her mind skipped desperately from one subject to another, looking for a lifeline to grasp hold of. Nothing good surfaced, and instead she found herself remembering the first time she had met him.

It had been at the airport in London. She had been feeling lonely and small, wishing for Aunt Joyce, for Jamaica and her friends, hating the father who had insisted on sending for her. Well, she had thought she hated him then, but boy, had she been wrong. There had been a sea of white faces everywhere, all hostile. She had known they hated her, and she had felt small, lost and afraid, and ashamed of her plaited hair as she had looked enviously at the smooth straightness of theirs. She had always wanted long hair, would have given anything for it, and she wished with all her might that her prayers would be answered and she would become like them.

She had been standing there, regretting bitterly that she had not stayed in Jamaica, when she had seen him coming towards her. His seemed to be the only black face in the tightly packed crowd, and she had wanted to run and hide as he came closer. A tall man, well over six foot, he had close-cropped African hair peppered at the sides with grey. His face had been handsome once, but now there were harsh lines biting deep into the sides of his mouth and his forehead. She had found the ugly glitter in the bloodshot eyes behind the thick-rimmed glasses frightening and had prayed for him to walk past. He hadn't, of course, and the blow had been a bitter one. She had always imagined her father would be a cross between Sidney Poitier and Richard Rowntree, not this nasty-looking man.

'Hyacinth!'

The sharpness in the voice brought her back to her present reality, and the fear she had been trying to suppress mingled with remembered horror.

'Yes sir?' she asked faintly.

'I think Joyce did give you too much freedom,' he said angrily. 'I not going to stand for none of this dumb insolence, you hear.'

'Yes sir,' she croaked hoarsely, desperately, swallowing hard.

'I hear you wet the bed again,' he said now, the eyes fixed unblinkingly on her.

'Y . . . yes sir,' she managed to get out in a frightened whisper, eyes falling, unable to stay averted.

'And you know what that means, don't you?'

She nodded, swallowing hard to try to force the blockage from her throat. He wanted to frighten her and she could see that he was puzzled by the lack of tears. She knew she would suffer for it from the way his hands tightened on the wooden arms of the chair. She could feel the shaking that she could no longer control, the sting of salt tears in a fresh wave behind her eyes.

'You know what to do, don't you?' he asked now. And the hands released the arms of the chair as the tears she had been fighting back started to flow. He was getting to his feet, and sick fear made her legs weak as she saw the lump in his trousers. The confirmation she had tried so hard not to see. Her tongue was large in her mouth, swallowing jerky and painful, and the tears flooded faster as the lump of his anger increased.

The shrill, high-pitched shouts of excited children's voices drifted across the bleak greyness of the concrete playground, as little groups of children ran about playing, not wanting to waste a moment of the morning break. Hyacinth stood in her customary position, huddled against the soot-stained wall of the science block, the biting cold causing her to shiver, a cutting wind making her eyes smart and run every time it blew in her direction. She could feel her teeth chattering of their own accord and prayed the break period would soon be over. She hated the cold, hated the crowded playground and the screaming, noisy children. It was hard to believe they were at least eleven, the same age as her. But then everything in this strange country was hard to believe. She hated Beacon Girls, and the thought that she was sentenced there for another four years was hard to bear. It was such a long time, four years of huddling against a wall shivering with cold and without friends, the only black girl in her year, whom not even the other black children wanted to know. She thought longingly of Jamaica, of her two friends, Florence and Cynthia. They had enjoyed their recess breaks, the three of them, walking in the school grounds, sitting under the big spreading Bombay mango tree. There was always plenty to talk about, plenty to plan . . .

'What you staring at?' The aggressive question brought her back sharply to the cold of the small, mean-looking playground. Hyacinth blinked uncertainly as she found herself looking into hate-filled green eyes. She had not been looking at anything; certainly not into the red-headed girl's strange-coloured eyes.

'I . . . I wasn't looking at you,' she stammered, bracing herself for the other to mimic her accent as the children were so fond of doing. The other girl had better things on her mind.

'Well, don't look again,' she said now, following the words with a sharp prod for emphasis.

Hyacinth had been looking down at her feet, hanging her head to emphasise her unwillingness to cross the other. Now her head flew up, mouth opening to protest. After another prod in her chest she clamped it shut, and her heart began to race with renewed fear. She shrank further into the wall, praying for the bell, hoping no one else had noticed. She had seen other black children picked on in this way, and an audience would surely cause the same thing to happen to her. She was hot now, the prickly heat of fear and shame blocking out the biting wind, and she almost cried out in frustration when from under her lowered lids she saw the crowd gathering.

She heard someone shout what sounded like 'Fight!' Her mind zig-zagged from the red-headed girl to the crowd that encircled her, was staring hate at her; then centred on the pain she knew must come.

'Kill the wog!'

It was a loud cry from somewhere in the crowd, but suddenly it didn't matter where, for it was picked up and flung back from everywhere.

'Kill the wog! Kill the wog!'

It echoed and re-echoed as the red-headed girl advanced on her again. Hyacinth edged to one side, eyeing her attacker warily. The red-headed girl was plump and a head taller than her, and Hyacinth knew she was a good fighter. She herself could not fight, had always been easy to beat, though at least she used to have friends who would back her up. It was this knowledge of her friendlessness that had kept her in a state of constant fear, and she avoided any conflict. But now she knew she was going to suffer, she just knew it. So intent was she on the other girl, she did not realise that she had reached the edge of the encircling crowd until a hefty push sent her sprawling. Then the laughter and abuse started. She looked up in time to see the red-headed girl reach her, foot raised to kick.

The children stood together in a semi-circle, shrill excitement in their raised voices, the sound drifting across the small playground, mingling with the dust and grime. The teacher on duty shook her head in amused tolerance, before turning briskly back to the inviting warmth of the school buildings. She was still smiling her amusement as she opened the door.

After the break was gym, and a silence greeted Hyacinth as she dragged herself into the changing-room, a smiling, sniggering silence that left her weepy with fear, and bowed under the weight of shame. She hated this lesson anyway, but today she could see that it would be worse than usual. She knew that Mrs Mullens, the PE teacher, disliked her, had done so since her first day. She had been late getting to the lesson, and had found everyone jumping over a strange box thing which the teacher insisted was a horse. Hyacinth had known she could not jump over it. Everyone else had bloomers under their short skirt; she did not. The teacher had ordered in vain, she could not bring herself to look so stupid. Not even the taunts of the other kids had made any difference. Try as she might, the thought of the shame of exposing her panties had been too much for her. She had tried to explain to Mrs Mullens, but the woman had simply got angrier.

'You blacks had better learn that you are in our country now!' she had snapped before ordering her to report to the headmistress. Of course she hadn't gone, and nothing more had been said about the incident. But it still lay between her and Mrs Mullens — that and her colour.

'OK, girls, let's have you.' Mrs Mullens had sprinted in, brisk as ever in her blue track-suit. Hyacinth tried to move along with the flow, hoping that she would be overlooked in the jostle.

'Hyacinth Williams!'

Hyacinth jumped, looked up guiltily at the mistress, as she came to an abrupt halt by the door. The others flowed round her, and soon she was alone, eyes fixed on the silver-coloured whistle dangling from the yellow ribbon round the woman's neck.

'Yes miss,' she said, as the woman stared disapprovingly down at her, arms folded across her broad chest.

'Look at me when I am talking to you, girl.'

Hyacinth raised fearful eyes to the icy-blue in the thin face.

'You have been fighting.' No question, just a bald statement of fact.

'No miss, I fell against a wall.'

The woman looked sceptical. 'And that is how you got a swollen eye and cut lip?'

Hyacinth's tongue ran nervously over her torn, distorted lip.

'Yes miss,' she mumbled finally, ashamed of the lie even as she spoke it. There was a pause in which the woman looked at her, eyes thoughtful. She opened her mouth several times as if to say something, changed her mind and closed it again.

'Well, in the future, try to watch where you are going,' she said finally, before adding, 'I suggest you go to the nurse so she can do something about your injuries.'

'Yes miss,' Hyacinth answered, turning away in relief. 'And Hyacinth,' the voice halted her, 'as you are in no state to do gym, you may come and watch afterwards.' She almost fancied the woman was sorry for her, and resented the concern. Mrs Mullens' voice intruded again, full of its usual sharpness.

'Margaret White! You are late again.'

Hyacinth turned to see the half-caste girl partially concealed

17

behind one of the changing benches. At Mrs Mullens' words, however, she shuffled forward into full view.

'I warned you about lateness,' the teacher continued. 'You will report back here at four o'clock for detention.'

Hyacinth had halted at the teacher's words, and now she looked at Margaret curiously, wondering how the girl would react. To her surprise Margaret was looking at her, her light-brown eyes full of anger and the promise of revenge. Hyacinth felt sick. Somehow Margaret White blamed her for what had happened. She couldn't understand it. How could it be her fault? Turning, she stumbled from the changing-room, almost blinded by tears of self-pity. What was she going to do?

Margaret White was someone she had been afraid of from the day she entered the school. A mixed-race child adopted by white people, she seemed to hate the black kids even more than the whites did. Hyacinth could remember the many humiliations the other girl had heaped on her, the times she had tripped her or pushed her over in the dinner hall. On top of that, Margaret had the reputation of being the worst bully in the first year. Hyacinth always went out of her way to avoid her. She had heard stories about red people at home, could still remember her aunt declaring to the neighbour, 'Well, you know how red neaga stay, dem is ignorant from dem born till dem dead,' after yet another incident involving one of the two red people living in the yard. One thing she knew, Margaret White was definitely red, from the tinge of her skin to her matted, uncombed hair. She wondered what the other girl would do to her. She might take pity on her, given that she had already been beaten up. She rejected the idea as soon as it formed. Margaret White wouldn't care how many times she had already been beaten. She was going to come after her as soon as she could.

It was after lunch, in the long stretch between eating and returning to class, that Margaret White found her. Hyacinth had abandoned her usual place by the science building for a more secluded spot near the kitchen, hoping she would be harder to find. None of the children usually came this way, preferring to congregate round the toilets where they could have a sly cigarette, safe from the prying eyes of inquisitive teachers. For a while no one came, and she had finally found the courage to venture out and ask the dinner lady the time. Once, twice, she did this, and now, with only fifteen minutes to go, she was beginning to breathe again. Her mind wandered off on her favourite daydream, picking it up at the same spot as the day before and every day before that. It was a good one, almost real, the smell of ripening mangoes, red- and yellow-coat plums slowly obscuring the rank smell of the cold playground. With her back against the kitchen wall, sheltered a little from the wind, it was almost warm enough to dream of green grass and bright sunshine. She imagined she was lying on the side of the long, deep gully, behind the tenement where her aunt lived, the long grass tickling her nose in the warm breeze, the clammy red and milk-white cherries rustling in the high trees above her head. If she stood very still she would not feel her cold thighs rubbing against each other, or the numbing, burning pain in her fingers. A shower of stones caused her to look up, and her heart sank as she saw Margaret White walking purposefully towards her, kicking the gravel underfoot as she came.

Hyacinth felt her dinner lurch alarmingly in her stomach. Her lip still stung, her body still ached from the beating of the morning, and she knew she could not take another one.

'You got me in trouble with old Mullens,' the girl said, coming to stand in front of her, looking threateningly at her. 'Thanks to you I got detention and me mum won't half kill me.'

Hyacinth felt panic bubbling up inside her. She searched frantically for something to say, some way of placating the other girl.

'I'm sorry,' she said finally, lamely.

The other girl snorted. 'What do you mean, sorry? You should go back to the jungle where you come from before I show you sorry.'

'I didn't come from no jungle,' Hyacinth defended warily, feeling hot and embarrassed by the other's assertion.

'Yeah? Then where you come from, a mud hut?'

A vision of the tenements with their zinc fencing and old rusting shacks, some with holes eaten right through, flashed shamefully through her mind to be pushed back hastily. 'I come from a city,' she said breathlessly, a little desperately. 'A nice big city with lots of sunshine and grass to play on at school.'

'Then why don't you go back?' the other girl demanded, thrusting her face right into Hyacinth's, spit spraying from her mouth as she spoke.

Hyacinth stood very still as she spoke, not daring to protest, hardly daring to breathe. 'My father brought me here,' she answered almost humbly, averting her eyes from the other girl's.

'Then tell him to send you back. We don't want no nigger here.'

'*You* can't call anyone nigger.' It was out before she could stop it and Hyacinth felt as shocked as Margaret looked, shock mingling with a tiny dart of pleasure as the other girl almost recoiled.

'What d'yer mean?' Margaret asked aggressively, thrusting her face forward again.

Hyacinth hesitated, backing away from the other, but as if her tongue had a life of its own, the words started to tumble out. 'Everybody know your father black and your mother dumped you when he run out on you, so that's why you live with white people. All the white kids laugh you to scorn behind your back.'

There was a silence and Hyacinth edged away, sliding across the join between the kitchen and the dining-room wall. Suddenly Margaret let out a bull-like bellow and charged at her. Hyacinth's heart leapt in her mouth, and she stumbled jerkily, jumping aside in fright. Margaret, off-balance, caught out by the unexpected movement, went straight into the wall. Hyacinth blinked unbelievingly as she saw the other girl straighten shakily. Her heart was racing madly, but now the fear had been joined by something that replaced the familiar shame and guilt that always followed a beating. She had moved, had got out of the way before the other girl could hit her, and she felt a sudden surge of hope, of confidence as the other girl lunged at her again. She was no longer thinking about what she was doing, and the pain from the cuts and bruises of the morning receded to the back of her consciousness.

This time she was ready for Margaret, who seemed to rely on a tactic of charging at her opponent, probably hoping to overwhelm her with her size and bulk. This time the bull-like momentum carried her straight into Hyacinth's fist, and Margaret reeled as a foot came out to trip her up. Hyacinth had learnt that trick well. It had been used on her so often, she now did it instinctively. Margaret crashed painfully to the ground and Hyacinth was on her in a flash. Her fists flew as she laid into the bigger girl, taking out all her pent-up frustration in a burst of angry destruction. She felt light and happy, as the other girl tried desperately to dislodge her and protect her face at the same time. She was beating

Margaret White, she, Hyacinth, was making the other girl cower the way she had cowered so many times before. God, it was good. She was so engrossed in what she was doing that her fists continued to fly even after she was lifted bodily and sent sprawling to one side of the prone form.

'Hyacinth Williams and Margaret White, what is the meaning of this?' The teacher paused, and when no answer was forthcoming from either girl — 'The bell went five minutes ago and now I find you fighting instead of in your classes.'

Hyacinth felt shocked at the news. She hung her head as the teacher spoke, eyes darting furtively around the playground, registering in shock that it was indeed empty and silent.

'Stand up, both of you, and answer me when I speak to you.'

Hyacinth scrambled to her feet, seeing Margaret doing the same out of the corner of her eye, not able to hide her satisfaction as the other swayed. She felt ashamed that she had been caught by a teacher, but still could not suppress her satisfaction, despite her knowledge of the woman's disapproval.

'I am waiting for an explanation of this disgraceful behaviour,' the teacher persisted, arms crossed, one foot tapping impatiently on the gravel of the playground.

'We were playing and didn't hear the bell,' Margaret said sullenly.

'Playing?' the teacher asked disbelievingly. 'Is this true, Hyacinth?'

Margaret glared at her, daring her to disagree, belligerent despite her defeat.

'Y . . . yes miss,' Hyacinth stammered, eyes sliding away from the woman's direct stare.

'Do you take me for a fool, girl?' the teacher demanded coldly.

'Yes . . . I mean no, miss.'

The teacher's eyes were impatient. 'You will both take detention this evening.'

'I already have detention,' Margaret said defiantly.

'Then you will come after that and take more detention,' came the cold reply.

'Please miss,' Hyacinth said tentatively, swallowing hard, heart racing, stomach suddenly sick with dread.

'What is it, Hyacinth?' The teacher was not encouraging,

obviously impatient to go. But Hyacinth plunged on, the spectre of her father's face with its evil grin rising to mock her. 'I can't take detention,' she said desperately, pleadingly. 'I have to get home, I just have to.'

'Are you daring to tell me when you can stay behind, girl?'

'But my father will expect me home, miss,' she persisted, near to tears.

'You should have thought of that before fighting in the school grounds,' the teacher said unsympathetically, adding briskly, 'Now run along before I double the period.'

Her heart was pounding as she hurried down the school corridor, wanting to run, yet mindful of the teachers' ever-watching presence, knowing the penalty of such an action. The clock on the wall showed twenty minutes to five. How would she explain her lateness? What excuse could she give? Her eyes prickled with tears as she imagined him sitting in his blue chair. She could see the impatience on his face as he checked his watch over and over again. He would be drinking barley wine as he always did, pouring out the last drop from each bottle, draining it carefully against the side of the glass. 'He'll kill me,' she thought, feeling sick and frightened, wishing she could go anywhere but to that house.

She picked up speed as she left the school gates, her feet scarcely touching the ground as she sped over the uneven pavement. She could imagine the anger growing in him and she was thankful that the school was within walking distance. She tried to increase her speed, the vision of him sitting there, that smile on his face, the evidence of his anger growing larger, forcing her to move even faster still. She was running faster and faster, head down, clutching her satchel to stop it banging against her side. Occasionally, she would stumble over a raised piece of pavement, and then she would swear under her breath. Words she did not even know she was aware of, words she associated with him in his moments of anger and annoyance. The dingy street leading to her road seemed endless, the pavement more cracked and uneven than usual. She felt hot and sticky despite the evening chill, and her head ached from the tension.

Then she was fitting the key in the lock, her hand shaking so much it took fumbled moments to get it right. Her breathing was ragged, her eyes blurred with tears of fear, and her heart nearly stopped when the door was suddenly wrenched open. Hyacinth's mouth opened to plead, and she slumped with relief when she saw the anxious face of her seven-year-old brother, David.

He wasn't there! She knew it straight away as she looked at the younger child.

'What do you mean by opening the door and frightening me like that?' she asked angrily when her racing heart had subsided a little. The little boy looked unsure. 'I'm sorry, Hyacinth,' he said penitently. 'Mam told us you would give us tea but you was such a long time we got upset.' Hyacinth pushed out of the way as she came through the door, eyeing him with dislike as he stumbled back awkwardly, watching in distaste as the prominent mouth, so like his mother's, began to tremble. God, she hated him. He looked just like a baboon and, God, was he stupid.

'Where's your mother?' she asked impatiently.

'She had to go back to work for a bit and she didn't come back yet.'

'Well, you and your brother better keep out of my way,' she said grudgingly, 'and you just have to wait for your dinner.'

The little boy looked upset, and his mouth trembled harder. 'I'm hungry,' he said tearfully.

'I don't care if you was going to starve,' Hyacinth snapped in irritation. 'You are just going to have to wait.'

'I'll tell Dad on you,' the child shouted in frustration.

'And I'll tell him I was cooking and you came in and started to play with the fridge.' Hyacinth smiled at the look of fear in his eyes, saw the guilt that told her clearly he had been in the fridge.

'At least I don't wet the bed,' he shouted, giving her a sudden vicious kick before skipping out of the way.

Hyacinth gritted her teeth. She wanted to hit out at him, to kick and pound as she had done this afternoon, indeed stepped forward before common sense and fear halted her. She knew what would happen if she did that; still had scars on her back to remind her. Instead she gave him a bitter look. 'Go to your room,' she almost screamed after him. 'Get out of my sight and take that stupid brother of yours before I really hit you!'

The little boy halted, looking uncertainly at her. 'I'm sorry,

Hyacinth,' he said tearfully. 'I didn't mean it, honest, is just that I'm hungry.'

'I said get to your room! Go on! Now!'

She gave him a push, coming forward again, and he ran off, looking fearfully over his shoulder as he did so.

'God, I hate them!' she thought bitterly after he had bolted up the stairs. 'I hate them all so much. Why can't they die, why can't they all die? I wish I was dead.' Struggling out of her thin plastic coat, she hung it up, standing for a moment feeling depressed, before turning reluctantly to the kitchen.

Two

She sat up with a start, a feeling of dread following her through layers of sleep into a reality of clammy wetness. The damp nightdress clung to her in increasingly cold folds every time she shifted. Her mind grappled with the problem. Rejected it. She told herself it was perspiration, that the nights were warmer and she was sweating in her sleep. Filled with dread, mingled with hope, her fingers groped, found and recoiled from a soggy wetness that no amount of perspiration could have brought. A shiver shook her as her nose gradually became aware of the smell of fresh urine all around her. She could imagine it seeping through the bed, penetrating the mattress till it gradually dripped into a pool on the worn carpet underneath, as it had done the last few times. Fear crawled in her belly as she thought of the morning, and she wondered what time it was. Eyes strained to pick up signs of tell-tale lightness in the impenetrable darkness of the room.

She prayed that night would never end, and that when she woke tomorrow it would be a dream and the bed would be dry, — anything but that she would have to face another stinging beating on her already tender back. Her heartbeat increased with the anticipation of what was to come, but she pushed it to the back of her mind, and slid down into the bed, curling round to avoid as much of the wet as possible. The more she tried to relax, the more her heart raced, while anticipation and fear made her mouth dry; but finally she slept, a restless sleep full of terrifying, nightmare images.

Morning found her waiting in fearful anticipation, unable to move, filled with horror at what must come. He was working nights that week, and the ritual of bed-checking would come soon. The sound of a key in the front door brought a wave of shaking to her limbs, and she lay there, unable to move, sweat breaking out all over her body. A few moments later, the bottom but one stair groaned as a weight was lowered onto it. She squeezed her eyelids closer together, breathing deeply as she had been taught in PE, hoping that this would slow her racing heart. Her mind followed the ritual up the stairs without thought. First to come off would be the large brown boots, laces carefully loosened. Then the socks. Then would come the sound of the stair settling as the weight was lifted from it. His coat would come off next, followed by the railway jacket he was so proud of. Last the red railway tie would be loosened, and the top two buttons of the grey shirt undone.

Now mind-image merged with reality and the stairs creaked slowly, each one nearer, each bringing a fresh wave of fear shaking through her body. She did not dare look up as the door was pushed open, but stumbled to her feet as he came into the room.

'This room stinks,' he said mildly, a humourless smile on his face. 'Did you wet the bed again?'

Hyacinth nodded, keeping her eyes averted from him, not trusting herself to speak. He walked over to the narrow bed, pulling down the blanket with a quick tug, exposing the brown-edged stain she had hidden in her shame.

'Why did you wet the bed?' The words mingled in her ears with the painful pumping of blood and ragged breathing. She kept her head bent, ears straining desperately, as if to pick up the blow before it landed.

'I don't know,' she said faintly, pleadingly.

'Don't know was made to know,' he said ominously.

Hyacinth felt the desperation bubbling up inside. How could she tell him how it was? How could she explain the dream, the dream that had haunted her for so long? He would never understand how it felt to get up in the middle of the night, to creep down the stairs, along the dark corridor, the glimmer of the street light casting long, monstrous shadows in her way as she darted through the kitchen, the strange wailing of the congregating cats the only sound to be heard. He could never understand what it was like to sit on the toilet, hands braced against the seat, feet pressed hard against the cold lino. Then came the straining, the pushing to get it over quickly, all the time holding back the fear that lapped at the dark corners of her mind, and lurked in anticipation somewhere out of sight, somewhere along the route she had come. It had always been like this. Fear driving her to hum songs to God, to mutter 'Get thee behind me Satan,' in a hushed and frightened voice. Aunt Joyce had always understood, but he never could. He would never understand her panic as it started to rise in warm wetness around her thighs, to run in rivulets down her legs. She could never explain the suffocating fear of waking to a freshly wet bed.

A stinging slap brought her sharply out of her thoughts, head lifting fearfully.

'I ask you if you don't have no shame.' His eyes had narrowed to slits, the smile replaced by a frown which multiplied the lines on his forehead, bringing a fresh wave of fear. She felt helpless in the face of the question. To say yes would be insolent, no, arrogant. Jumbled, half-formed sentences raced through her mind, mingling with her pounding heartbeat which seemed to echo there.

'This dumb insolence has got to stop,' he said ominously and Hyacinth tensed in readiness for the next blow. Time seemed to drag, agonising seconds in which she dared not look at him, wished she had the courage to run, or at least to fight back.

'Strip the bed and tell Maureen you are to have a cold bath.'

Hyacinth hid her surprise, keeping her head averted; he was going to let her off. Yet the hope just born was short-lived as he continued, 'And when you finish, I want to see you in the front. And Hyacinth,' — he had been walking towards the door, but now he stopped — 'don't let me have to come for you.'

It was later, the numbness of the cold bath still deep in her fingers and toes, that she pushed open the dull pink door to the lounge. Down in her stomach she could feel the beginnings of the shaking he always inspired and, as she closed the door, she felt it spread. She had to clench her teeth to prevent them chattering as she stood stiffly in front of his chair, knowing from experience that to betray fear was to invite early punishment. He was drinking barley wine even this early, and a wave of hate and disgust made her clamp her teeth together harder. Two years she had watched him drink that stinking brew, two years of beatings and mistreatment, and she was sure that same barley wine had been the cause of some of it. She had read somewhere that you couldn't drink so much without becoming violent.

'I am not going to beat you today.'

Hyacinth blinked in surprise. Her mind had been painstakingly avoiding acceptance of the beating to come, and now she found she was safe after all.

'I am going to take you to the doctor,' he continued. 'Something must be wrong with you, for you to keep bed-wetting like this.'

Hyacinth nodded eagerly, fear pushed to the back of her mind in the sudden relief. Why hadn't she thought of that? Of course something was wrong with her. Nobody wet the bed, not at her age. She wondered if she would have to go into hospital, have an operation maybe. It would be nice to get away from him, especially as a girl at school who went there once said that all the nurses were Jamaican.

'If the doctor say nothing wrong with you, God help you!' he warned. She didn't care about that, she knew there was something wrong with her, that the doctor would say as much. At least now the beatings wouldn't be so frequent. There would be less excuses to find for curious schoolmates and prying teachers asking about the raised red weals and broken skin on her legs, arms and back. Then she was free to go and, as she closed the door, relief flooded her. She took the stairs two at a time, not noticing the skinny woman at the top until she almost collided with her.

'Your father he never beat you, eh?' There was malice in her eyes as she reached out to give Hyacinth a vicious pinch. 'You think he like you, make you get away with it? Well you do anything and see if he going to let you off so easy.'

Hyacinth shrugged off the bony hand, pushing impatiently past the woman. 'Why don't you get lost, you big-eyed toad,' she said in sudden anger, as the other reached out and cuffed her.

'What did you say?' the woman asked angrily, eyes glittering with spite. 'Say that again and see if I don't tell your father how you insult me. Then is he you will have to deal with.'

'Tell him what you want,' Hyacinth said indifferently, walking away with head held high, not even trying to hide the smile on her face. She knew he hated Maureen as much as he hated her. After all, why else would he beat her, and in front of his friends too? The only thing he would punish her for was hitting the woman. What she said to her was their business.

She had not always been so bold with Maureen, of course. Once she had been almost as afraid of her as she was of him. At first when stung to respond, she had waited with pounding heart for him to hear of it. Yet nothing had come of it. She soon realised that as long as she was not rude to Maureen in front of him, he didn't care what she did. Sometimes, when her conscience troubled her about her disrespect, she would remind herself how much the woman hated her. Maureen had made her hatred known from the start, had announced her intention of getting Hyacinth out from the day the girl walked through the door.

Hyacinth remembered those first days with bitterness, remembered Maureen telling her that her two children were the only children of the house, and she, Hyacinth, only there on sufferance. God, if they only knew how much she wanted to leave that bleak, unhappy house. How much she longed for the sun-bleached cheerfulness of the grey wood shack that had been her home for the first eleven years of her life. How different it had been from this peeling, black-painted house full of fear and hate. Now her whole life seemed to be one endless round of work and fear, cleaning, cooking, beating and bed-wetting. It had been so nice with Aunt Joyce, who had always understood, had never treated her badly. She had been popular, with lots of friends. No one had teased her, taunted her. Now her only happiness was sleep, for that was when she could go home again and take up her interrupted life.

It was peaceful in the brown-carpeted surgery, most of the hard grey chairs empty in the silent waiting-room. Hyacinth sat quietly beside her father, hardly daring to move for fear of attracting his attention, willing her knees to stop shaking. She couldn't understand it. How was it that her knees shook even when he was not about to beat her? Straining her ears to try and pick out words from the murmur of voices coming from the partially open door of the doctor's surgery, she tried to judge how long the fat woman who had just gone in would be. It was her turn next, and she couldn't wait to escape from his company. It seemed like forever, but finally she found herself being ushered into the room by a large, white-coated nurse, her father following close on her heels.

'Hyacinth Williams,' the woman announced as she opened the door, and she walked in on a wave of importance, her father temporarily forgotten in the thrill of hearing her name called so officially.

'What can I do for you?' the doctor asked, when father and daughter were both seated on chairs facing his desk. To Hyacinth's surprise, her father took off his cap, looked servile.

'Hyacinth keep wetting the bed,' he said respectfully. 'This two year since she come to England, she wet the bed non-stop.'

The doctor looked at the notes on the desk in front of him, but made no comment.

'She is thirteen last birthday,' Mr Williams continued awkwardly after the pause had stretched on for some time, 'and I feel something wrong with her.'

'Have you taken her to a doctor before?'

Mr Williams shifted uncomfortably. 'No, I thought she would grow out of it,' he said defensively. 'Is only 'cause she getting worse that I decided to come.'

Hyacinth squirmed in the seat beside him, feeling the prickly heat of shame rise in her face, sting on her back, cause her scalp to itch, as the doctor turned his gaze on her.

'What happens when you wet the bed?' the doctor asked, his voice reassuring.

'I don't know,' she mumbled.

'Speak up when the doctor speak to you!' The voice, like the crack of a whip, caused her to jump and fresh shaking to start in her body. She had not expected that from him, here.

'Mr Williams, perhaps it would be better if you waited outside,' the doctor suggested quietly.

'I don't think so, doctor, you don't know her like I do. Hyacinth is a liar,' Mr Williams blustered. 'She refuses to tell the truth and I have to watch her.'

Hyacinth felt the sting of tears and she stared hard at her hands, trying to force the tears back, not wanting the white man to see her cry; not daring to do so anyway, with her father there.

'I am sure I can detect lies from the truth,' the doctor said coldly, dismissively.

'But you don't know her, sir. You wouldn't be able to tell, she so good at it,' Mr Williams persisted, and Hyacinth curled her toes in her shoes in shame.

'Nevertheless, I would still like you to wait outside,' came the reply.

Once he had gone, Hyacinth felt herself relax, some of the tension leaving her.

'Are you afraid of your father?' the doctor asked suddenly.

Hyacinth stiffened, mingled pride and fear warring with a sudden hope. 'No,' she mumbled finally, reluctantly, eyes sliding away from him. She would never dare tell him that her father had warned her about white people — how they hated black people, how they would trick them and kill them. Even at school she saw that — how the black kids were treated, how she was treated and, if she needed more evidence, look afraid how he had been of this man. No, she mustn't tell him anything.

'Does he hit you when you wet the bed?'

'No.' She shifted uncomfortably as she repeated the lie.

'In that case, why were you trembling when he was here?'

She could not answer that, could not bring herself to admit the truth, not to this man, not to anyone. They would take her away, kill her, and then no one would ever know. The doctor changed tack. 'Did you wet the bed before you came to England?' She shook her head vigorously. After all, one or two accidents could hardly be called wetting the bed.

'What caused you to do it here? Are you afraid of the dark? Is that it?'

'It's not that . . .' she said, trailing off. Then, taking a deep breath, she plunged on before she could think about what she was saying. 'If I knew it was going to happen, I would never let it,' she blurted out.

'So how does it happen?'

'Sometimes when I wake up the bed is wet, and sometimes I

really think I am on the toilet. I sit on the toilet and it doesn't seem to stop coming down. Then when I wake up the bed is wet.'

The doctor thought for a while. 'Do you wet yourself in the daytime?' he asked gently.

Hyacinth looked shocked. 'No!'

'Do you think there might be something wrong with you?' he persisted.

She raised her shoulders uncertainly, not quite sure what to say. 'I think maybe there is,' she said finally.

'Are you homesick? Would you like to go back to . . . Jamaica?'

Hyacinth nodded eagerly, heart leaping with sudden excitement, sudden hope. No wonder he was asking questions about Jamaica. She was glad she had told him now. Perhaps he would suggest that the only way for her to stop wetting the bed was to go back to Jamaica. Maybe he would say she was sick because she had to leave her aunt. Oh boy! she couldn't wait. She would be home soon. Home and safe.

'Can you wait out in the waiting-room,' the doctor said briskly, 'and tell your father to step back in for a few moments.' Hyacinth smiled happily at him. Boy, this would be good. Her father was obviously afraid of the doctor, he wouldn't dare refuse to do what he told him.

He came out of the surgery looking angry, and he gave Hyacinth a long look, before turning and marching for the door. Hyacinth hid her satisfaction behind the blank mask she had learned to assume, but inside her the happiness was bubbling up. No doubt the doctor had told him to send her home. Yes, he would be angry about that. He hated changing his plans and when she was gone there would be no girl child to keep the place clean. They travelled home in silence, she struggling to keep up with his long stride, often stumbling over the cracks and missing paving stones.

All that evening and the next day, she waited with quiet expectation, finding new energy for her work. At school she stood in her usual spot against the wall, a now familiar figure that the others had finally allowed to be alone. She was used to being friendless now, two years of daydreaming making her even glad of it. She knew she dare not make friends, even with those black children who wanted to. She could never take them to her house, could never invite them round with the casualness that they flung invitations back and forth between each other. So she chose to be alone instead, gaining a reputation for snobbery that she hated but had learnt to cultivate. The occasional taunts from the white children had long ceased to hurt; and now she hardly even heard them, her mind centred firmly on going home. She was so happy, sometimes she thought she would burst if she didn't tell someone. But there was no one to tell; so she whispered it to her friends in her dreams, to her aunt, satisfying the need to share. In the evening her feet no longer dragged along the concrete, instead they sped along. Now she wanted to go home, wanted to get back to hear the news she had waited for so impatiently.

By the time he left for work on the third day after her visit to the doctor, she had started to lose hope. Tears of frustration burned at the back of her eyes as he walked past her without a word. 'He wants me to suffer before he tells me,' she thought bitterly. 'But I won't let him see it. He have to send me home in the end, the doctor told him so.'

That night she dreamt she was already home. First she was in the plane above the clouds that stretched motionless like bits of suspended cottonwool all around her. Then the pilot was announcing their arrival at Kingston Palisados. The rest was a blur of movement until Aunt Joyce folded her into her large, warm embrace. Hyacinth pinched herself to make sure she was there, that this was not another cruel dream. There was no pain, but who would expect it when she was so happy? Aunt Joyce had on the same blue dress and straw hat she had worn to put her on the plane when she was eleven. In fact, everything was the same. The orange seats in the airport lounge, the noise of the planes outside, and the glare of the hot July sun outside the wide picture windows.

'Hyacinth, child, how you do?' Aunt Joyce asked, holding her away from her finally.

'Oh Aunt Joyce, it's so good to be home,' she said, happiness bubbling inside her.

'You just in time for the Independence celebrations,' the woman said, picking up the battered brown grip that had held all Hyacinths's possessions when she had left for England.

'Your father tell me that you come back for good.'

'Yes, and I'm never going to leave Jamaica again,' Hyacinth said, skipping happily along beside the other's reassuring bulk.

'Oh Aunt Joyce, I missed you all so much. I thought I would never see you again.'

'Well, you here now, chile, just put it behind you and live now,' her aunt said, swinging the door open for her to go through.

She felt the cool breeze as they boarded the bus. It rustled the grass, trickled across her back, down her legs. Now the bus was moving along the Palisados. The cool wetness of the sea breeze bathed her body through the open window, the noise of the wind whipping the words from their mouths. Hyacinth strained to catch what her aunt was trying to tell her, striving to understand her agitation; but it was not until they had left the sea road and turned towards Kingston that the words became clear.

'But Hyacinth, how you get so wet?' her aunt asked, putting out a plump hand to feel the white cotton dress.

Hyacinth looked down at herself in surprise, feeling the drops of moisture against her skin. 'I don't know,' she said, looking puzzled, feeling suddenly anxious and upset.

Her aunt was looking angry, the good-natured features suddenly contorted with rage, the large hand raised, threatening, no longer soft and reassuring. One stinging blow was followed by another and another, leaving her bewildered, disoriented, half-way between sleep and wake.

'Get up!'

She moved groggily, jerkily, limbs still heavy with the remnants of sleep, body heavy with residual tiredness. Yet fear moved her, caused her to stumble in an inelegant scramble from the bed. Cool air made her shiver as the damp folds of the nightdress clung to her.

As awareness seeped into her consciousness, so did hope. He would have to send her home now. He wouldn't dare to beat her, not after what the doctor had said. She could feel his anger, did not dare to look at him in case she saw evidence of it. And she had to struggle to control her fear, doctor or no doctor. 'Whatever he does, it will be worth it,' she thought desperately. 'At least he will have to send me home now.'

'You think you bad, eh?' he asked, rolling up the sleeves of his grey work shirt. 'You think you is a bad woman?'

Hyacinth swallowed hard, trying to dislodge the lump in her throat. She had to force herself not to turn and run, knowing from experience what that would bring, his present anger less than that which any defiance might bring. She opened her mouth to say something, anything so as not to be accused of dumb insolence, but only a weak croak came out.

'So you are not going to answer me, eh? You feel you big and bad. You forget, Hyacinth. Getting rusty. I going to have to knock some of the rust off you.'

She shifted in distress, eyes going to the smile on his face, throat locked in fear.

'We going to see how bad you are. Come, man, come downstairs and let we see if you can remember who is boss in this house. I have just the thing to knock the rust off you!'

She wasn't even aware of the tears running down her cheeks. All her attention centred on the raw pain in her throat, and the pain which was to come. Shivers were beginning to reach out from the pit of her stomach, to her arms, her legs, everywhere. He was standing by the door, holding it open for her. She wished he would go first, that she could tell him how afraid she was to go ahead of him. Instead she stumbled forward, avoiding the grim smile on his face.

The kick when it came was not unexpected, yet the blow to the small of her back was so savage it lifted her off her feet. She saw the top of the stairs appear, rush forward at frightening speed. She grabbed instinctively, clawed out for the banister, caught it, held on for an endless moment, fingers slipping along the smooth, worn wood. Then she was falling, the bottom of the stairs rushing to meet her. She heard the thud long before she felt the pain of impact, was dazed before the breath was knocked out of her bruised and shaken body. For a long moment she lay in stunned surprise, feeling weak, heart racing and lurching crazily.

'Get up!' This time the kick was between her shoulder blades, and she instinctively raised her hands to protect her face.

'Nothing no wrong with you,' he said savagely, prodding her with his foot. 'So you better get up before I make sure you can't.'

Somehow she managed to stumble to her feet, legs shaking as much with reaction as fear. 'I'm going to die,' her terrified mind screamed silently. 'I'm going to die, and they won't even know he killed me.'

He pushed her into the front room, moving past her to his chair, pulling the strip of tyre out without bothering to lift the seat cushion. 'Why did you wet the bed?' he asked, easing his bulk into the chair, tapping the strip of tyre gently against his trouser leg. She watched the movement of the tyre, unable to tear her eyes away.

'It was an accident,' she whispered finally, chokingly.

'So you think something wrong with you, eh?'

Hyacinth nodded with relief. Maybe he was not going to hit her after all. Maybe he was just angry that the doctor had stopped him from beating her.

'I didn't hear you,' he said ominously.

'Yes,' she whispered, hands clenched at her sides, praying that he was only trying to frighten her.

'And it isn't laziness?'

'No sir.'

'Or spite?'

She shook her head.

'And you not afraid of the dark?'

Again she shook her head.

'You mean the doctor was lying when he tell me all these things?'

Hyacinth's heart lurched, then raced on. The silence seemed to stretch on, the ticking of the clock loud and ominous in her ears.

'I ask you a question. Was the doctor lying?'

'No sir,' she whispered, the dryness of fear mingling with the numbness of resignation in her mouth.

She lay between the cool, clean sheets, the unaccustomed feel of the dry nightdress nice against her skin. It was lovely to feel clean, not to feel that slippery wetness, the itchiness of stale urine between her thighs. She was glad the punishment was over, though her shoulders smarted and her head still ached where she had banged it against the bottom stair. At least that sick feeling would not have to stay with her all day.

The door crashing inward made her heart stop, and she sat up in apprehension, thinking that he had somehow come back to beat her again. She almost felt relief when she saw her stepmother's spiteful face instead.

'What do you mean putting your wet sheets in the wash, without me seeing it first.'

Hyacinth slumped back against the pillow, ignoring the woman.

'You must think you big,' the woman said, and her stomach clenched at the echo of her father's words, yet she kept her face blank, staring ahead as if the other did not exist.

'When your father come in and I tell he bout this, you going to find out how big you is.'

'He already knows,' Hyacinth said sullenly.

The woman sounded gleeful. 'You mean he check your bed before he go to work?'

She nodded wearily. Let Maureen have her fun; after all, she got beaten as well.

'Did he beat you?'

Hyacinth looked up at the expectation and glee on the other's face with disgust. Maureen was sick, always wanting to know about her punishment, always happy when she heard the details.

'Yes,' she said shortly.

'He obviously didn't beat you enough,' Maureen said angrily, when Hyacinth continued to stare at her with sullen dislike. 'You must forget is plenty things you can catch your tail for aside from bed-wetting.'

Hyacinth felt the hate bubbling inside her, and she had to clench her fingers in the mattress to stop herself lunging for the protruding eyes. She remembered all right, everything that went wrong in the house was blamed on her. If her stepbrothers broke anything, her stepmother always made sure she got the blame for it.

'You better mend your ways,' Maureen was saying. 'I don't want a girl chile telling me what an what not to do. And you know if anything happen and I tell your father is you, he go beat.' She shrugged. 'Is up to you if you want that or not.'

Hyacinth ignored her, forcing herself to stay where she was, not to lunge at the other. She knew the threat was not idly made, but nothing she did would change that. Maureen would die before she allowed her children to own up to anything. She saw nothing wrong with using Hyacinth to protect them. Maureen was always threatening her, bargaining for respect, but she knew from long experience that it would be a one-sided thing. She wished the woman would go, wished she would just disappear. She was the cause of most of her misery, always searching for something to report, always prying.

'You better get up and do the breakfast,' Maureen said now, seeming to tire of baiting her. 'And if I was you I wouldn't put a foot wrong, or your father going to hear about it, sure as I stand here.'

Three

She sat alone in the cold room, barely registering the fact that her fingers had long ago lost all feeling, premature darkness wrapping her in its shadowy cloak. The greyness was kind to the worn furniture and fading wallpaper, turning the room into insubstantial unreality. Outside, white flakes of snow drifted silently past the old-fashioned glass in the rotting window-frame, breaking their even flow only when a gust of wind blew them into a flurry.

Hyacinth huddled further into the inadequate warmth of the thin acrylic cardigan and stared morosely through one of the cracked panes of glass. Her mind was split between the cold, soft whiteness outside and the constant burning itch in her toes. It was a feeling she had lived with for a long time, the discomfort and pain with her in both her sleeping and waking hours, the need to scratch an ever-present thing. Her third winter in England and she wanted to die. She was so miserable, so unhappy, and so cold —always so cold. Her eyes moved from the window, to rest longingly on the paraffin heater that she had been forbidden to use. She thought of the warmth locked out of reach, felt resentment at the fact that she was never allowed to enjoy it. Everyone else could be warm, her stepmother, stepbrothers, father: everyone else but her. No wonder her swollen feet itched, no wonder they went from blocks of ice to raw, burning pain.

She tried to remember what it had been like to be warm; tried and failed. Warmth was something now associated with the night, when the heat from her body finally seeped into the cold cotton sheets, which then cocooned her in a safe world, filled with sunshine and happiness. The heat of the summer past was all but forgotten; that of Jamaica more enduring yet still confined to the region of the night, retreating with the dawn, taking familiarity and comfort away. In the daytime, only cold, fear and the constant maddening itching was reality. She gritted her teeth as once again a wave of irritation made her want to scream with the need to scratch. Her feet, like bloated, well-padded cushions, jerked spasmodically, her scalp prickling in sympathy as she waited for the wave to ebb.

Outside, the drifting snow had turned into a purposeful fall, cloaking everything. It caused the day to darken, the temperature to fall a little more. Hyacinth huddled further into her cardigan, eyes once more seeking the heater. She wished with all her heart that she dared turn it on, but rejected the idea again. Her stepmother would have checked the level of the paraffin. She would be sure to notice. The flickering light of the falling snow caught her eyes, and she turned back to the window. She found herself watching the flakes in fascination, trying to make out their patterns as they rested briefly on the glass before melting away. She was not quite sure when she noticed the sensation of floating upwards off her chair. A feeling so unexpected, like the one she sometimes got when she closed her eyes and lay face down on her bed. Hyacinth closed her eyes, startled by the unexpectedness of it. The feeling dropped from her, a switch turned off. She looked again, curious, a stab of excitement deep within her as it happened again. 'It would be good if I could just float away, not stopping till I got home,' she thought wistfully, as the feeling seemed to carry her higher and higher. Her eyes smarted from the effort of not blinking, when she finally looked away. 'It's only make-believe,' she told herself sadly, her mind groping for words to describe the experience. Still, she could not stop her eyes from drifting back to the fading light outside, the ever-increasing fall of snow. It was nice just to sit there and forget the evening to come, even though there would be hell to pay if she did not finish the housework before her stepmother returned.

It was two weeks since she had last gone to school, two weeks since she had been able to stuff her feet into the flat plastic shoes her father told her still had wear in them. They had pinched and burned the toes of even her normal-sized feet, and she had wept when they had lasted well beyond the summer, defying all attempts to wear them out. Her heart lurched as she remembered the ugly smile on his face when he had come in from the night shift to find her still at home. He had been working overtime that week, and her heart sank as she heard Maureen talking to him in a low voice as soon as he came through the door.

'What wrong with your foot, Hyacinth?' he had asked her in a voice which made her feel sick with fear. She had stared dumbly at him, not daring to say anything. Oh, she knew what it was all right. But she knew he would blame her, blame her and punish her. She had heard other children whisper about verrucae, even knew of some who had been forbidden to go swimming or take a shower because of them. He moved restlessly in front of her, impatience in his face as her mouth moved, tried to form the answer. The slap across her face sent the words scattering in her head. Fear prevented them re-forming.

'I ask you a question.'

Her head sang from the force of the blow, and tears of self-pity and fear stung the back of her eyes. No one had told her that a verruca could spread so quickly, could leave both feet shapeless and swollen, itching and burning.

'You feel you big? You think you don't have to answer?' They were in the front room, and now, rather than wait for an answer, he strode over to his chair and pulled the strip of car tyre out. Hyacinth felt her heart beating in her throat, her teeth threatening to chatter against each other.

'No please!' she cried in panic. 'I wasn't feeling big.'

'Then what wrong with your foot?' he asked again, slapping the tyre gently against his leg.

'I have a verruca,' she said hastily, the words stumbling to get out.

The unexpected sting of the rubber across her back made her jump, her racing heart making her breathless and weak.

'You trying to be smart?' he asked, lashing out with the tyre again.

Hyacinth cowered, catching a stinging blow across the back of the hand she had thrown up to protect her face: 'I h . . . had a verruca a . . . and it spread,' she said desperately. The tearing, smarting feel of damaged flesh made her back quiver in reaction, unable to brace for a follow-up blow.

'I going to knock some o' the lie from you, girl,' he said now. Hyacinth felt the familiar terror seeping in, and her whole body shook as he ordered, 'Go take off your school uniform, it cost money and a don't want it to stain.'

Her heart was hammering as she stumbled through the door, eyes going longingly to the street door only steps away, mind rejecting the idea almost before it formed.

'You father going to teach you a lesson.'

Her head had turned to find her stepmother regarding her gloatingly, but she had brushed past the woman, too frightened even to find a reply.

A sudden gust of wind rattled against the ill-fitting window, seeping through the many cracks so that it could have been blowing inside. Hyacinth tensed herself, the throbbing in her feet telling her that another wave of itching was on its way. A darting movement caught her eyes, distracting her, and she watched idly as a little brown bird hopped delicately from one mound of snow to another, pecking gingerly as it searched for food. She felt a sudden wave of envy as the bird suddenly soared effortlessly into the sky, disappearing into the greyness. She loved these afternoon times when her father was on the late shift. It was good just to sit, despite the cold. Good not to have to always be on the move, always busy.

Somewhere in the distance, a clock struck four. Hyacinth's heart stopped, then skipped crazily along. She had not meant to sit down for so long. Her stepmother would be home soon and the dinner was not even started. The large pile of ironing the woman had left stood heaped across the room in silent mockery. She could almost see the spiteful glee in the yellow face as she looked at it. Easing herself cautiously from the chair, she cast a quick distasteful look at her shapeless feet in the thin grey socks. Even her slippers, an old discarded pair of her father's, no longer fitted; and a piece of string held them tied to the bottom of her feet. Partly in an effort to stop the slippers curling and partly as a result of the size of her feet, she walked with an ungainly shuffle, and she felt a quick stab of shame at how she must look.

A week later, Hyacinth woke to a cold grey dawn and the

knowledge that she was lying in something wet and sticky. As the implication seeped into her consciousness she came fully awake, heart racing with dread. It was nearly two weeks since she had last wet the bed, and this time she had not even had the dream. Struggling to sit up, she stared apprehensively at the door. He was on mornings this week, and soon he would be getting up. She sat there shivering in her nightdress, too full of despair even to move. It was only after she had been there for some seconds that she became aware of the painful ache in her pelvic region. It was a heavy, dragging kind of pain that only her fear of punishment could have masked. Her head had begun to ache, and a wave of self-pity suddenly engulfed her. She wanted to cry, to curl up and disappear. Instead, she lay back down in the bed, ignoring the discomfort of it. Pulling the blankets up around her, she snuggled into their warmth, following the instinct to blot out the unpleasantness that was to come, her mind drifting away from the shame and the pain.

They were playing high-jump with a thick piece of vine from the nearby gully, the boys stripped to the waist, the girls baking in the thin cotton frocks they wore. Hyacinth had volunteered to hold one end of the vine. She was no fool, the high-jump looked painful, lots of jumpers grazing themselves as they landed heavily on the coarse sand. All she really wanted to do was to lie under the shade of the clammy cherry tree, watching the sun glinting through its leaves, feeling the warm breeze brushing the strands of hair that escaped from the cane-row plaits her aunt had done so carefully the night before which tickled the back of her neck with their white ribbons. She knew the others would force her to join in, maybe even to jump. So she stood patiently holding one end of the vine, enjoying the shade and the breeze as best she could. She consoled herself with the fact that her side was under the shade of the only tree in the tenement yard.

They must have been jumping for nearly an hour when the grey-looking boy with the patch of ringworm at the side of his head volunteered to take her end of the rope. Hyacinth's heart skipped a beat. She hated the ringworm boy with his grey-black skin and his runny nose, and she wished he wouldn't keep coming near her.

'You go jump and mek me hold this end,' he persisted when she ignored him.

'No man, I like holding and anyway Aunt Joyce say I can't get dirty today.'

The boy hissed through his teeth: 'Cho! you just fraid fe try. Bwoy Hyacinth, you is a real coward.'

Hyacinth ignored him, willing him to go away, but the other children had taken up the chant now: 'Coward! Coward! Hyacinth is a coward.'

The ringworm boy grinned nastily, and she shifted uncomfortably under the combined taunts, finally driven to deny the jibe. 'Prove it! Prove it!' they screamed now, and she wished she had never opened her mouth. There was a rising feeling of apprehension in her stomach, a churning sickness that increased as she walked reluctantly, feet dragging, to where the group of jumpers stood talking and laughing in the sun. Her fear increased as they parted, cleared a space for her. Then she was running. She had to make it, had to jump that rope. It came towards her looming larger, higher from this side than it had seemed when holding it. She willed her legs to spring, to leave the ground, but then the rope was there and she had skidded to a halt instead. Three times she ran between the line of children, getting hotter, pain increasing every time. The harsh, biting sound of mocking laughter burned in her ears, merciless as the heat of the morning sun. She could not bring herself to jump that rope. Try as she might her feet refused to leave the ground, knowing the painful bump that waited for her on the other side. Sweat was running down her face, under her arms, trickling down her back. Her scalp prickled with heat and shame, while her feet burned and felt swollen from constantly pounding the hard ground.

This time she had to do it, had to stop the laughter before the soreness in her feet got worse, and the stitch pain which made her thighs weak caused her to stumble. As the rope loomed in front of her, she gritted her teeth with desperate determination. This time her legs left the ground and she leapt, higher and higher, higher than even the best jumper. Everything was forgotten in that moment of triumph as she soared down to land on the other side. The others came running, crowding round her in admiration, and she even managed to smile at the scowling face of the ringworm boy. It was nice to be the centre of attention. Nice to see admiration instead of mocking contempt for once.

'Jump again! Jump again!'

The cry echoed and re-echoed as the earlier mockery had done. She was eager to comply, wanting to prolong their approval as long as she could. Once again she soared above the rope and the feeling was good, freedom mingling with achievement, making her smile in triumph. It was then that she had landed. An inelegant thump, limbs flailing, one foot twisting in awkward protest. The pain was awful, blotting out even the cruel, taunting laughter of her so recently admiring friends. Now the pain was moving from her foot, spreading to her pelvis, an awful throbbing pain that dragged her back to the sticky reality of her father's house.

The door opened as she sat up, and her stepmother walked in, spite in her eyes as she took in the girl's worried features.

'You wet the bed?' she asked eagerly, almost smacking her lips over her protruding teeth.

Hyacinth sat feeling miserable, not bothering to confirm it.

'Get out and let me look,' the woman said impatiently, grabbing her arm with bony fingers.

She would have liked to pull out of the bony grasp, but fear and misery made her struggle out of the bed instead. The stickiness was worse when she moved, and she felt sick with shame. She kept her head bent, not wanting to see the tell-tale yellow stain on the sheet, cold causing her body to clench in the thin nylon nightdress. Her stepmother's angry exclamation caused her head to jerk up, and her eyes widened in horror as she stared at the exposed sheet. Where she had been lying was covered in blood, and a quick glance down at her nightdress revealed the same red.

'Oh God! Oh God I'm dying!' Hyacinth thought, panic bubbling up inside her. The pain in the lower part of her body increased as the thought swamped her.

'I suppose you know what this means,' her stepmother said coldly, mouth compressed with disapproval. 'I suppose you realise I have to tell your father.'

Hysterical fear bubbled up inside her. Of course she realised what was happening. She was dying, wasn't she? Bleeding to death, and now this evil woman was going to make sure she got punished for messing up the sheets. She stood there, eyes glued to the stain on the bed.

'Oh God, please don't make me die. I'll never want to die again!'

her mind screamed out. She became aware of a trickle between her legs, knew its stickiness to be the stickiness of blood. In that moment she hated the yellow-skinned woman enough to kill her too. Hate and fear mingled in her, and she suddenly launched herself at the woman, the pain and the swelling in her feet forgotten, swamped by a greater need. Hyacinth was a skinny girl, but hard work had given her a wiry kind of strength and Maureen could not dislodge her as she started to claw at her face.

The woman screamed, mouth opening on a wave of bad breath to expose decaying teeth. Hyacinth didn't care. All the pent-up frustration she had been feeling exploded as it had done once before. She felt satisfaction as the woman crashed to the floor in her effort to dislodge her, and she held on, clawing at the yellow face with determination. Everything else was forgotten, even the fact that her father was somewhere in the house, maybe even in his bedroom across the landing.

The man lifted her effortlessly, practically flinging her to one side as he ordered his wife to get to her feet.

'What happen in here?' he asked angrily, as Maureen staggered up.

'Lawrence, I come to wake Hyacinth and find she start to menstruate. Then she just up an attack me. A tell you, she mad Lawrence. You have to do something about she.'

'Shut up, Maureen,' the man said impatiently. 'I want to know what Hyacinth have to say bout that.'

Hyacinth knew from experience not to contradict the woman in front of him. She stood there, head hanging, heart beating sluggishly. The silence lengthened, the cold air and the tension causing shivers to trickle across her skin. Her feet were throbbing and the pain in the lower part of her body seemed to increase by the minute.

'Go and have a bath,' her father said finally, surprising her by not pursuing the matter. Her head jerked up, and she was relieved to see that the smile was not on his face, that he was not even angry.

It was not until she was in the bath that her real predicament came back to her. How could she be bleeding like this? What could have caused it? One thing she knew, it had to be serious. Why else would he pass up a chance to beat her? And the strange lump that appeared every time he had an opportunity to beat her had not even been there. A knock on the door caused her to slip automatically down into the warm water as her stepmother came in.

'A sorry about this morning,' the woman said, her voice unsure, almost nervous. 'But your father, he ask me to talk to you.'

Hyacinth ignored her, not caring what she had to say, hardly even noticing the wariness with which the other watched her.

'Do you know what menstruation is?' the woman asked, after an uncomfortable silence.

Hyacinth nodded, just wanting Maureen to say what she had to and go.

'Well, that's what you doing.'

Hyacinth bristled. How dare she! 'I don't do things like that,' she said angrily. 'Anyway I hear it make you blind.'

The woman looked startled, shifted in embarrassment.

'Is a different thing than that,' she said, her voice strained. Hyacinth shrugged again, knowing she was right, but too worried to argue the question. 'Every girl when they reach a certain age see a period,' Maureen tried again. 'She bleed for four or five days every month, and sometimes she get a bit of pain.'

Hyacinth was listening now; she might have disagreed about the amount of pain, but she was certainly glad to hear the rest.

'I know about periods,' she said, relief flooding her. A lot of the girls at school had periods. She always envied them as Mrs Mullens would allow them to skip showers. She hated the communal shower, hated having to step naked and defenceless along its length, her blackness exposed for all to see, to snigger about behind her back. She knew they did it, though they were always careful to hide it from her.

She was so wrapped up in her thoughts she hadn't heard the rest of what Maureen was saying. All she knew was that she was not dying after all and now she too would be excused showers.

'I'm going to fetch you some sanitary towels,' the woman said. 'And every time you see your period, I will let you have some more.' She walked towards the door, hesitated, coming to a decision. 'You must watch your father,' she said in almost a whisper, looking round nervously as she did so. 'You old enough for him to trouble you like he did with your cousin.'

Hyacinth stared blankly at her, wondering what was the matter with her. The woman flushed a dull red under the yellow skin.

'Your cousin left a book when she went. A didn't read it but is something to do with what happen to she.'

She looked as if she had said too much, glancing nervously around as she turned and hurried from the room. Hyacinth scratched the dry scalp at the back of her head, through short coarse hair. She was puzzled by what the woman had said. She often wondered about the mysterious cousin who had lived in her father's house, but she had been forbidden even to mention her name. Now she wondered what her stepmother meant by her father having troubled her. She wished she could ask someone, but she knew it would cause a beating. At the same time she couldn't understand how he could get any worse. As far as she could see, he was always troubling her, and Maureen was the chief cause of her trouble, with her lies and tale-telling.

She was drying herself when the woman returned, and she watched as she showed her how to wear the towel on the strange elastic belt.

'Don't tell your father I talk to you,' Maureen said, thrusting a book in her hand when she had finished.

Hyacinth looked down at the book, *Cider with Rosie*. What a strange title for a book. She wasn't even sure she wanted to read it. She felt light from the knowledge that she was only seeing a period, and important in her new belt and towel, despite the discomfort.

Her father's attitude changed subtly after the incident at the beginning of her period. He now encouraged her to spend less time on housework and, to her surprise and secret delight, often criticised his wife for working her too hard. She did not know what had caused the change in him and she did not think it would last, but she intended to make the most of it. *Cider with Rosie* lay at the bottom of her drawer, unread and half-forgotten.

She was back at school now, and in the lighter atmosphere at home, she found it possible to spend time in the evening trying to catch up on some of the two months' work she had missed. In her heart her one ambition remained constant, steadfast – to return to Jamaica. She knew it was expensive, her father was always saying how much he had spent bringing her to England. At the same time he was always saying that education was the only way to get rich.

She had decided that she would get education, lots of it, and then she would be able to return to Jamaica. She was not quite sure how it worked, but she intended to think about that when she had to.

It was about a month after returning to school that the first sense of uneasiness had come to her. She had taken to splitting the time before bed into homework and extra work to catch up. This night she had more homework than usual and worked longer than ever. The knock on the door was tentative and furtive, and she frowned in annoyance at the interruption. 'I hope she don't want to talk again,' she thought impatiently, head still bent over her book, thinking it was her stepmother. Since the period incident, the woman's attitude had also changed. Now she treated Hyacinth with a wary respect and even tried to speak to her on occasions. Hyacinth suffered her, but in her mind the years of bitterness stood between them.

'You should be getting your beauty sleep, not filling your head with books.'

Hyacinth's heart lurched, then raced with fear. She scrambled hurriedly to her feet, dropping the book in her haste as her father walked into the room. He had obviously just come from work, and was wearing the grey shirt and red tie of his job.

'I was just going to bed,' she said nervously.

'You don't need to be fraid bout me, you know,' he said softly. 'I not going to hurt you.'

She nodded uncertainly, tensing herself in case he was just testing her. Since coming to this house three years before, she had learnt to smell trouble, and now her instinct told her she would be better off anywhere else but there.

'Come downstairs and keep me company,' he coaxed. 'Is lonely to just sit by yourself. You can make me some tea, and wait till I drink it.'

She would have liked to say no, but she had no illusions about his response, his moods were too changeable to predict.

She brought the tray into the sitting-room, and put it hastily on the coffee-table beside him, hoping that he would allow her to go to bed. He was sitting on the settee, and now he patted the space beside him. 'Come sit here and talk to me.' She went reluctantly, sitting stiffly, praying he would let her go, fear moving inside her, making her body want to shake. 'Don't be nervous,' he said, making no move to drink the tea she had poured. 'I just want to talk to you.' His voice became insinuating. 'A father and daughter talk.'

She shifted uncomfortably, not knowing what to say, dreading an accusation of dumb insolence and the blows that would follow it.

'What do you know about men and women, Hyacinth?'

She did not like the way he asked the question, the intimate note in his voice, but at the same time she was relieved he did not seem inclined to hit her.

'Only what Maureen told me,' she answered hastily.

'Do you know what a man's body look like?' he asked suggestively.

'No, sir,' she answered nervously, not liking the way he was speaking.

'Call me daddy,' he said automatically. 'I am tired of telling you that. I don't want no man to take advantage of you,' he continued. 'So I going to show you some of the things not to let men do.'

Her heartbeat was making her breathing hard, she knew this was wrong, that he was going to hurt her somehow.

'Please sir, I already know what not to let men do,' she said in alarm, her stepmother's words coming back to her with sudden meaning. 'Don't let your father trouble you,' the woman had said, and she suddenly felt that this was what she had meant.

Her words took him by surprise, and his face was suddenly angry.

'How you know?' he asked in annoyance. 'Who show you?'

'Nobody,' she said, scrambling to her feet in fright as he reached for her. He was up, towering over her, eyes protruding and boring into her in his anger. 'You dirty dog. You bitch,' he said, hitting her hard across her face, fingers curling into a fist to repeat the blow. 'You think I don't know how you fling your tail at the boys on the street?' he demanded, advancing on her again, fist crashing down to send her sprawling.

Hyacinth was terrified. She had never seen him like this before. She could not think what she had done, what she had said, and her mind was too panicked to think. All she knew was that the lump in his trousers was larger than ever, while her face already ached and stung from the blows. When he bore down on her again, she cried out, frozen where she was, fear shaking through her. The sound stopped him in his tracks and to her amazement he looked furtively at the door.

'Ssh, don't make so much noise,' he said hastily, anger suddenly replaced by wary caution, the evidence of his anger reducing in size. 'You'll wake Maureen,' he added, 'and you know what that mean.'

Hyacinth nodded. She did not know what it meant, of course, but at that moment she would have agreed to anything to stop him attacking her again. She was on her feet now, and she stood there, shaking in front of him. He looked at her in disgust. 'I don't know why you had to do that,' he said in annoyance. 'Go on, get out of here. Maureen probably wake up by now.'

The next day she read *Cider with Rosie*. It was a good book, not particularly enlightening, but someone had ringed a phrase with black ink: 'Incest flourished where the roads were bad.' The phrase was to stick in her mind, fascinate her. She became obsessed to find out what it meant, looked up incest in the dictionary, read as much as she could about it.

She knew that her schoolwork was suffering as a result. The other children nudged each other and whispered about the books she read. Even so she couldn't stop. The more she read, the more alarmed she became. 'Incest flourished where the roads were bad' – surely her father would never try something like that on her. She wished she could be certain, could understand more of what she read.

It was inevitable that the teachers would finally notice her inattentiveness, and one day her English teacher spoke out in exasperation. 'Hyacinth Williams, you will stay behind after class.' Hyacinth felt sick. The last lesson of the day and she had to get into trouble.

The classroom emptied rapidly, everyone rushing out eagerly. Hyacinth sat where she was, nodding to those who muttered a hasty goodnight, avoiding the sympathetic glances of others. 'Hyacinth, what is the matter with you?' the teacher asked as soon as the door closed on the last child.

'Nothing, Miss Maxwell,' she answered, looking down at her hands.

The teacher looked disbelieving. 'I am not just talking about today,' she said gently. 'I am talking about your whole stay in this school. I realise that it must have been hard for you to adjust, coming to a strange country, but it is three years now, and I am sure everyone has tried to make you feel at home.'

Hyacinth said nothing. If she only knew, she thought sadly. She wished she could tell the teacher what it was really like being in England, but shrugged off the idea. She was probably like all the rest anyway, deep down underneath it all.

'I am aware that you have a far from satisfactory home life,' the teacher persisted when she failed to answer, then after a pause, 'I would like you to feel that you can confide in me, if you need someone to talk to.'

Hyacinth wanted to die of shame. She looked everywhere but at the woman, feeling sick with embarrassment. Mrs Maxwell knew what her father was like. How? How had she found out? Who had told her? The questions tumbled through her mind and her palms felt clammy. She had to struggle to keep her face blank, to stop the tears of shame from falling.

'There is nothing to tell, Miss Maxwell,' she said finally, wondering who else amongst the teachers knew about her father, intending to deny it at all cost. 'I am sorry I didn't pay attention,' she continued, 'but it had nothing to do with . . . home.'

Miss Maxwell looked sceptical. 'The other girls tell me you don't mix, that you don't have any friends.' Hyacinth shifted uncomfortably. How could she tell the woman what it was like? Everyone else had nice parents. She saw one or two of them sometimes when she was shopping with Maureen, and she felt ashamed of her stepmother, her ugliness, the fact that they thought she was her mother. She could never invite them to her father's house overnight, to sleep in a bed that smelt so strongly of mould and stale urine. And because of that she could never go to their houses, so she could have no friends.

The teacher was tapping her fingers impatiently against her desk. 'It's my personal choice, miss,' Hyacinth said stubbornly.

'Are you sure that is all there is to it?' The teacher's kindness reached out to her, begged to be confided in. Miss Maxwell was one of the few teachers who had always been nice to her, and she felt the words burning on her tongue. She had to bite down hard, fingers clenched, to prevent the truth spilling out. She wanted to talk badly, to share her feeling of being trapped with someone; but suddenly her father's words came to her – 'You think you get bad treatment here?' he often asked. 'Well let me tell you, if you run go tell the white teacher them going to take you away.' She had felt her heart leap with hope the first time she heard this until he explained. 'They don't like neaga in this country. All them white people smile up them face with them plastic smile, and then when you trust them, them kill you.' She looked at the woman warily, fancying that she was looking at her with hatred, plotting her death. She felt sick with fear, trapped, sandwiched between the hate and spite of the white world and the dark dingy evil that was the house of her father.

'Well, Hyacinth?' The teacher's voice made her jump, and she shifted uncomfortably.

'It is my own personal choice,' she repeated.

The teacher shook her head. 'Very well,' she said in a resigned voice. 'I cannot force you to confide in me if you do not wish to, but I hope that you will reconsider the decision not to.'

Hyacinth nodded in relief, glad that the teacher was letting the matter drop. 'Yes miss,' she said quickly.

The teacher looked undecided as if she intended to pursue the subject, and Hyacinth held her breath. She must have decided against it, for she suddenly rose to her feet: 'Very well, Hyacinth, you may go,' she said briskly.

Four

After the talk with Miss Maxwell, Hyacinth was careful to pay attention at school. Her father seemed to be keeping away from her since the incident. She told herself that black men did not do things like that. There had been nothing about them in the books she had borrowed from the library, and slowly, gradually, she pushed it to the back of her mind, reasoning that it was best to concentrate on getting to Jamaica, away from the threats and madness of England.

She had managed to put the whole incident aside, when he started to watch her bathe. Hyacinth hated these times. She would sit in the water, dying from embarrassment. 'Wash yourself, girl,' he would say, and she would hang her head in shame, as she scrubbed the top part of her body, praying he would leave before she had to stand up. Many times he would order her to stand up and wash, and the knowledge of the lump in his trousers would force her to obey. She hated her body, felt shame at the wisps of black hair that had started to grow on her pubic area and the fact that her breasts had started to swell. Sometimes she dreamt of asking him to leave, of telling him she found his presence uncomfortable, but it was only a dream, of course; she never found the courage.

Her stepmother seemed to avoid her eyes even more, watching her worriedly, but looking guiltily away if she caught her eye. Now she no longer tried to speak, and Hyacinth had the feeling that the woman felt sorry for her.

It was on a Friday, some weeks after her detention, that Hyacinth was called by her father. She had just returned from shopping with Maureen, feet dragging as she pulled the heavy trolley along behind the woman. The dim light spilling through the dusty glass of the front door warned her that he was in, her stepbrothers having been forbidden to turn the hall light on. He was in the front room, and the clink of bottle against glass told Hyacinth that he was drinking the inevitable barley wine as she paused to close the street door.

They were in the kitchen, unpacking the trolley, when he walked in with the exaggerated deliberateness that told her he had been drinking long. 'Hyacinth, I want to talk to you in the front,' he said insolently, propping himself against the door jamb.

'Lawrence, leave the girl alone!'

Hyacinth looked at her stepmother in surprise. Maureen had never dared to contradict her husband before. 'I see the way you keep troubling the girl,' the woman continued. 'What are you trying to do? You never going to satisfied?'

Mr Williams looked stunned, Maureen's outburst throwing him for a few moments. 'Keep out of this, woman!' he blustered finally, angrily. 'When I want advice bout how to treat my daughter, I'll ask.' He looked her up and down with dislike and contempt. 'You keep telling me that Hyacinth is not your concern, so just keep your mouth to yourself.'

'When I say that, was before you start cast your eyes at she,' Maureen said defiantly. 'For shame Lawrence, she is your own flesh and blood.'

Mr Williams' eyes seemed almost to jump out of his head in his anger, the pupils looking evil and dangerous. Maureen, arms folded, by the cooker, took an involuntary step back as he moved towards her, but still persisted. 'If the government find out what you do to Anne you would be in prison now, Lawrence. Hyacinth is your daughter, man. You can't do this thing to her.'

Hyacinth looked at the woman curiously, willing her to continue. It was tantalising to hear about this Anne, never finding out what this thing was that had been done to her. She imagined it was connected with the trouble Maureen had told her to watch out for. Maureen did not continue. Instead, she backed a step, as the man came towards her again.

'Say that again.'

Maureen looked frightened, but this time she stood her ground, repeated what she had said. Her voice shook as she spoke and she winced when he grabbed her skinny forearm. Hyacinth looked on in fascinated horror, wondering what he was going to do.

'Get out of here. Go to your room,' her father told her without turning round. She hesitated, not sure what to do. 'Get out!' he bellowed, incensed by anger and drink. 'And keep your brothers out of here if you know what good for you.'

Hyacinth stumbled out, afraid he might turn his anger on her, mindful that it was she he had come to fetch. Closing the door with shaking hands, she winced as she heard the thud of the first blow landing, followed by Maureen's scream. Maureen always screamed from the first blow, and kept on screaming right through. She hesitated again, torn between helping the woman and doing as he said. Her hand was on the door knob, turning it, when common sense reasserted itself. After all, what could she do, except maybe get a beating herself? Maureen had got her into enough trouble in the past, let her get some of it back now. Still, she was in two minds as she walked hesitantly away, and as the woman's screams got more desperate, she actually started to retrace her steps. The sound of a door opening made her heart stop and for a second she actually thought he had caught her, before it dawned on her that the noise had come from behind. Still shaken, she whirled round to see her two brothers peering round the front-room door. She glared at them in dislike, bundling them back into the room, feeling guilt at their fear. 'Stay in there, and don't come out,' she warned them, 'or you will be next.'

Long after she had closed the door on them she stood in the passage, seeing the fear in the little boys' faces, the tears in their eyes. She bit her lip, looking hesitantly at the kitchen door, from where the pitch of the screams had increased. The continuous thud of blows connecting with flesh made her feel sick, and she pressed her stomach with her hands.

'Maybe I should get help,' she thought desperately, looking longingly at the street door, wondering if she dared. Only fear of what might happen stopped her. She listened, curiosity mingling with fear. She wondered if that was how she sounded when he attacked her, bitterness washing over her at the thought of how many times she had suffered because of Maureen.

'Let her suffer,' she thought in sudden anger, self-disgust mingling with her bitter memories.

Turning defiantly she ran up the stairs, refusing to allow the guilt to swamp her, thinking only of the pain the woman had caused her. Yet the screams stayed with her, sounding terrifying as they rang out without pause through the cold and dingy house. She fancied the screams were aimed at her, accusing her, pursuing her to her room. They rose up through the floorboards, the woman's desperation transferring itself to her, as she lay cowering on the narrow bed, head buried under the lumpy pillow.

A knock on the door brought her out of her private world of guilt. She was surprised to find that the noise had stopped, it had been so loud and real in her ears. She sat up reluctantly, turning apprehensively to the door as it started to open. He had come for her, he had finished working on Maureen and now he was ready to start on her. The thoughts ran through her head, increasing her fear, as the knock came again.

'Come in,' she said, wishing she could just tell him to go, body shaking in remembrance of her stepmother's screams. He had never beaten Maureen so badly before. What was he going to do to her?

The door was pushed open, and her relief was physical as she saw David's head push cautiously around it. He looked frightened, his face more like his mother's as he came to stand in the room. 'Mam say if you like you can come with us,' the little boy said nervously. 'Mam say we have to leave or Dad will kill her soon.' Hyacinth felt a stab of guilt as she saw him standing there, trembling in front of her, guilt mingled with shame. She had not gone to Maureen's aid, and yet the woman was offering to help her. She pushed the thought aside impatiently, as the little boy stood in front of her hopping nervously from foot to foot. 'Why should I feel guilty anyway?' she asked herself in annoyance. 'She caused me enough trouble, it's time she got some of it back.' She knew why the woman wanted her to come. It was three years since Maureen had done any cooking or cleaning and she no doubt intended to keep it that way. Well, she wasn't going to fall into that trap. For all she knew the woman might even give her over to the white people. No, she wasn't so stupid as to go with them.

The little boy still stood where he was, looking more nervous and frightened by the minute.

'Tell your mother I wouldn't go anywhere with her when I know how she hate me already,' she said to him now.

The child looked dejected: 'Mam said to tell you to please come. She say you won't be safe any more and she don't want nothing to happen to you.'

Hyacinth felt the smile widening the sides of her mouth.

'Boy, she must be really frightened,' she thought gloatingly.

'I certainly don't intend to come with you,' she repeated, feeling satisfaction as the tears started to slip out of the child's eyes. 'As far as I'm concerned the whole lot of you can drop dead.'

She heard them go soon after. Maureen's voice came to her, thin, high-pitched with fright as she hurried her children out. The front door closed furtively on them and Hyacinth shook her head. He knew they were going all right, had probably told the woman to leave. There was no way he could sit in the front room and not hear them go. Her suspicion was confirmed by the heavy tread on the stairs almost as soon as the street door closed. Hyacinth's stomach muscles tightened with fear at the thought that he might be coming to beat her too, and she wished desperately that she had gone with them. There was nobody else there now, only her. All her triumph at Maureen's downfall dissolved in fear of him, and she sat frozen on the side of the bed as the door was pushed open.

There was a smile on his lips as he came through the door, and the bulge in his trousers seemed extra large.

'Come downstairs and make me some coffee,' he said, and the way he looked at her made her feel frightened and embarrassed. She wished she had the courage to stay where she was, wished she had taken the chance and gone with Maureen. Bad as the woman was, she was not frightened of her.

He was watching the television when she took the tray in, lounging back in his chair, a glass of barley wine in his hand. Aside from exchanging the glass for the coffee and telling her to sit down, he ignored her until the film was finished. Then, 'Come here, Hyacinth,' he said coaxingly. She hesitated, wishing that she dared to refuse, regretting bitterly not having gone with her stepmother. Her legs shook as she got reluctantly to her feet.

'Come on. A not going to hurt you,' he said encouragingly. 'I want you to sit with me.' He pulled her down on his knee, and she sat stiffly, feeling awkward and embarrassed as his arms went round her. 'You getting to be a big girl now,' he said, bouncing his knee gently up and down, and giving her a squeeze at the same time. Hyacinth shifted uncomfortably. 'Y . . . yes, sir,' she said nervously, tensing for the blow when she saw him frown.

'You always find it hard to call me Daddy, don't you?' he asked.

She nodded warily, surprised that he had not shouted at her at least.

'Well, if you don't want to, you can call me Lawrence,' he said reasonably. 'The two of us is all alone now, so we have to be company for one another.'

She nodded, fear making the blood drum in her ears. She would never be able to call him that. She wished she could get off his knee, wished she had more courage, enough at least to stand up to him on this issue.

He fell silent and she sat rigidly, hardly daring to breathe.

'Do you have a boyfriend?' The words made her jump, shift nervously.

'N . . . no. I don't,' she said awkwardly, heart hammering against her rib cage even harder. 'God, please, please don't let him do what he did to Anne,' she prayed silently. She could feel the anger bulge growing in his trousers under her, and she felt terrified, sick. What had she done? How had she annoyed him this time? She wasn't sure what frightened her most. The thought of a beating, or the nameless thing done to the faceless Anne that was so terrible, he could have gone to prison for it.

She could feel panic bubbling up inside her as she continued to sit on the evidence of his anger. 'I . . . I am . . . tired, can I g . . . go to bed, please?' she stuttered, before she could think about it. Her heart was racing with the strain.

He looked at her in surprise and then she was stumbling to her feet. 'You not going to give you Daddy a goodnight kiss?'

She froze to the spot, not knowing what to do, what he meant. She knew that nothing could force her to go near him again, not tonight.

'N . . . no, sir,' she said, shifting uncomfortably, bracing herself for the punishment that was to come.

He shrugged, picking up the half-empty glass of barley wine. 'All right. Go to bed then.'

She needed no second bidding, diving out of the room as fast as she could, trembling with fear and reaction.

Later, huddled under the blankets in the narrow, stale-smelling bed, curled up to the hot-water bottle so recently belonging to one of her stepbrothers, she wondered how she was going to cope with him. She felt sick and apprehensive at the thought of living with him on her own. The more she thought, the more she regretted that she had not gone with her stepmother. At least she knew how to deal with the woman. The fear of what had been done to Anne plagued her. Try as she might, she could not imagine what it was, and she prayed again that he would not do the same thing to her.

'Hyacinth, wake up.'

Aunt Joyce was standing there big and impatient, irritation causing lines on the good-natured face. Hyacinth looked at her, blinking owlishly. 'You forget what day it is, chile?' She sat up suddenly, memory returning, the worry that had been like a nagging toothache receding to the back of her mind. 'No, Aunt Joyce,' she said, excitement bringing her wide awake as she scrambled out of bed. How could she forget this day? She had waited impatiently for it all week. Today was Saturday, and they were going to Dunns River Falls. She had never been to Dunns River before. Now she would not have to envy the others at school who had gone. She rushed over to the small wardrobe, pulling out clothes with careless haste. She had been to the beach before — Gunboat Beach with its line of almond trees was only a short bus-ride away. Often they would cook dinner and walk down the narrow mud lane to where the bus stopped. Hyacinth would always ask for the window seat. She would sit with her nose pressed against the glass, watching as they passed the Palisados, and later staring in fascination at the men who her aunt told her were convicts, hewing endlessly at the white cliffs. Once there she would climb the almond trees, biting eagerly into the fleshy fruits, carefully storing the seeds to break and eat later. She would run into the waves, screaming with excitement as they rushed towards her. But all those things were nothing compared to what she had heard about Dunns River.

Hyacinth heard the roaring of the waterfall long before the shaky country bus rattled to a halt, and she shifted impatiently, wanting to be off, to see it for herself. She could see the water spray from where she was, and she wondered what it would be like to stand under it. The whole day spread in front of her, bristling with possibilities, and she hated the waste of even a few minutes. She thought they would never get there, but finally she was wading into the creamy surf, the green water almost transparent as she bent to look at the small fish darting round her legs. The breeze was warm and wet, the sea comforting in her ears, it stretched endlessly, as far as she could see. Here and there she could see boats skimming past, looking hurried and out of place on the lazy sea. She had left the Falls till last, wanting to prolong the anticipation. But now it beckoned her, no longer to be resisted. She felt the blood racing through her as she watched its waters tumbling down to the beach and into the sea. Glancing back, she saw that her aunt had taken out her crochet, a cane-cutter's hat firmly on her head, while her bulk rested comfortably against the bole of a coconut palm.

She turned to skip back towards the Falls, but suddenly water was all around her. It felt clammy, smelt unpleasant, like fresh urine. Fresh urine! The thought registered, shocked, pulled her from the vivid peace of the sunlit beach to the dark, clammy reality of soggy sheets, and the lonely silence of the English night. She lay shivering, fear seeping into her. Her heart was pounding uncomfortably and she felt sick. 'What am I going to do?' she asked herself urgently, the sickness coiling in her stomach, hands shaking, palms slippery at the thought of punishment to come.

Change the sheet! The thought was so loud, she fancied it had been spoken. She lay there undecided, heart hammering. Dare she? Would she have the nerve? Supposing she got caught? Supposing he got up before she finished? Yet she could not stop thinking about it. What did she have to lose anyway? she argued. She would get beaten if she got caught, but she would also get beaten if she did not try.

Her heart was pounding so hard when she got out of bed, she had to stop and take deep breaths, ears straining in case he had somehow heard the noise. The even breathing from the partially open door across the landing reassured her. But her heart raced again when a loose floorboard creaked as she stole down the stairs, the sound like an explosion in the silence. She groped along in the dark, too frightened to put a light on, sure her heartbeat was as loud as it sounded in her ears. She had never done anything like this before, and her body had broken out in a cold sweat by the time she reached the bathroom.

Back in bed, mattress turned over, clean sheets and nightdress, she felt sick with reaction and lay shivering with fear at her own daring. She fancied he had heard everything, that he knew of the mattress slipping, falling onto the springs with so much noise. Maybe he was going to wait until morning and then confront her with his knowledge. She was sure her guilt must show, positive that she still smelt of urine, that he would know as soon as he walked through the door. He would kill her if he ever found out what she had done. She lay there, feeling clean and dry, shaking with terror.

I got away with it! She could hardly believe it, repeating the words over and over again, as she watched him gather his lunch things and go through the door. Now she had seven hours to get rid of the evidence, and she had it all planned. Racing to his room, she quickly stripped the bed, before running to get the sheets from under hers. The smell of stale urine rose with them, and she wrinkled her nose in disgust. 'I'll never wet the bed again!' she vowed fiercely. She felt disgusted. Fourteen years old and still wetting the bed!

That night he told her he was going out. Hyacinth bent her head so he could not see her happiness. She had been dreading another night like yesterday; now she felt light with relief. After he had gone, looking unfamiliar in a smart black suit, she felt such a sense of freedom that for a few minutes she just sat in the front room doing nothing. It was nice just to sit there and plan her evening, work out how she was going to spend this precious time.

She heard him come in hours later, his stumbling steps and irritated cursing waking her up. Hyacinth tensed, listening to the noise downstairs. He sounded annoyed, as if the night had not been successful. She prayed that he would find nothing wrong, no excuse to take out his frustration on her. She only relaxed when she heard the front-room door close, knowing that he would be drinking for some time, that he had found nothing wrong.

She awoke again, drifting up through layers of sleep at the sound of his footsteps on the stairs, and her heart nearly stopped when he halted outside her door. When it opened and the light came on, Hyacinth froze, heart hammering. She fancied she could hear the sound of the car tyre, that he was raising it, ready to bring it with tearing force across her back. She cast her mind around desperately, trying to guess what she had done. The salt taste of sickness poured into her mouth. Had he found out what she had done this morning? Did he somehow know that she had wet the bed? The thoughts chased through her head, and she was shaking when he pulled the covers off her.

She was too frightened to pretend sleep, and she sat up quickly, knowing he would punish her either way. He had taken off his jacket and loosened his tie, and there was a dark stain where he had spilt drink on the white shirt.

'You feel all right, Hyacinth?' he asked, after looking at her for a while.

She blinked owlishly against the sudden light, feeling surprised. He walked over to her, depressing the side of the narrow bed as he lowered his bulk onto it.

'We must get this room decorated,' he said casually.

Hyacinth nodded, feeling uncomfortable, the cool night air making her shiver in the thin nightdress.

He rested a grimy hand on her chest. 'You getting to be a big girl now,' he said, leaning forward, the smell of stale alcohol making her want to be sick. She swallowed hard, praying he would leave quickly. She felt a sudden, overwhelming need to go to the toilet, had to press her thighs tightly together to force it back. She would have liked to have told him, but did not dare.

'You not listening to me.'

Hyacinth's heart skipped, her concentration still centring on the need to go. 'I have to go to the toilet,' she gasped, scrambling off the bed in desperation.

Mr Williams looked put out as she stood there jiggling about in front of him. 'Go on before you wet yourself,' he said, anger and frustration on his face. 'And don't dare let me see you wet the bed. I going to know how you do it if you do.'

As she raced from the room and down the stairs she could hear him swearing angrily, the crash of his door slamming shut.

'Hyacinth!' She stiffened, clutching hard at the plate she was drying, putting it down with shaking hands, and turning down the gas under the rice carefully before going to see what he wanted. Since Maureen had left, all she ever seemed to do was run around for him. It was worse, much worse now, and once she got home she never had any time for herself if he was there. She could not remember him being so demanding before. He was always finding reasons to get her to come close to him. She always felt nervous now, not missing the fact that the lump of his anger was there, permanently.

Pushing open the front-room door, she hovered close to it. 'Go to my room and bring my glasses from the bedside table.'

Her heart sank. She could see his glasses clearly on the table beside his glass, but she dared not point this out to him. 'Go now!' he said impatiently, as she hesitated.

She was halfway up the stairs when she heard his heavy tread behind her, and her stomach muscles clenched. Quickening her step, she wondered miserably if he was angry at her hesitation. She knew she had to get there before him, could not allow him to accuse her of insolence again. As she had known, there were no glasses on the bedside table. She stood undecided in the middle of the room, not daring to go, wondering with a sinking heart if he had drunk too much. She could hear him approaching, and her heart-beat increased with every step he took. She bent her head, clenching her hands, mind casting desperately about for an excuse she could give why the glasses were not there.

'Come here, girl. I've got something for you.'

Tears of self-pity flooded her eyes, seeped under the lids, tracing a path down her cheeks. She bit back the pleading words, knowing they would only make things worse. Yet try as she might, her feet refused to move, and she braced herself for the sting of the strip of tyre. She heard him move, and when his hand came down on her shoulder she jumped with surprise, heart racing.

'A not going to hurt you, Hyacinth,' he said, pushing her towards the big double bed.

'You better watch your father.' Maureen's words came back to her as the man pushed her down on the bed. It was then that she saw the lump in his trousers, no longer hidden. Exposed. Large, obscene, frightening.

'Incest flourished where the roads were bad.' The words leapt into her head, caused her heart to race faster. He was coming closer, closer.

Hyacinth rolled aside, panic scattering her thoughts, fear bubbling up. 'So that's why Maureen used to make the little hurting cry,' came the unbidden thought. One thing she knew, whatever he was going to do with that thing, it wasn't to her. He was not going to trouble her. She was not going to be like Anne.

She scrambled off the bed. Made a dash for the door.

'Come here, Hyacinth,' he bellowed angrily. 'Come fore a take the skin from off a your back!'

She hesitated, years of fear stopping her. He lunged at her, his big hand closing round her arm. Hyacinth felt sick with terror, her heart was beating in her throat, choking her. Her scalp and armpits prickled madly. Somewhere in the distance she thought she heard Maureen screaming, the sound long, terrified and unending. It was only the savage blow across her head that made her realise that the sound had been coming from her.

His rough hands were fumbling with her blue school skirt, while his whole body seemed to be shivering, his breathing rasping and obscene in her ears. She could feel his hand pulling at her panties, while his breath, rancid with stale liquor, was in her mouth, in her

62

nose, travelling down her throat, making her retch, her stomach churn in protest. Now she could feel the lump rubbing against her belly, and she heaved, the sickness bubbling up, salt liquid pouring into her mouth.

'Incest! Incest!' The word drummed in her ears as she felt his hands pinching and pawing her. The tears were burning furrows down her cheeks as she felt him move above her, his weight pinning her, pushing the breath from her body, suffocating her. She felt the lump moving, and she pushed and struggled, clawing out at him, her head singing as he slapped it about in annoyance. Now he was shifting on top of her, weight lifting, her legs no longer trapped. She could hear him grunting as he struggled with his trousers, felt herself shrink as he grabbed one of her hands. She moved in panic, legs jerking spasmodically, hitting hard against him, and her heart nearly stopped as he crumpled across her. She pushed at his heavy weight, rolling across to leap to her feet as he struggled up, cursing and swearing as he staggered towards her. Hyacinth let out a frightened cry and dived for the door. Then she was running, running and crying, stumbling on the stairs, shielding her head with one hand, pulling up her panties with the other.

It was a stitch in her side that finally slowed her down. That, and the continuous tears that burned her eyes and threatened to blind her. She had run about half a mile, and she could see the trees of the park near her school silhouetted against the clear night sky, behind the weathered grey wood fencing. She stood still, heart hammering, body shaking, breath coming out of her in rattling gasps. She took great painful gulps of air desperately into her lungs, eyes continually darting in the direction from which she had run.

The air was still cold at night, despite the mildness of late spring, and as the cold seeped into her, Hyacinth realised that she didn't even have her school jumper on. The breeze was icy as it blew against her skin. She knew she could not stay there. Knew she could not go back. 'And the roads wasn't even that bad,' she thought sadly, sitting on the low wall in which the fence was embedded. She wondered where Maureen was, wished with all her heart that she had gone with her. She supposed she really should do something, get in touch with someone. She knew that she did not need money to phone the police, just had to dial 999; but the thought of doing that frightened her almost as much as going back.

'They don't like neaga here.' The words came back to her, echoing in her head every time she tried to build up the courage to make the call. Instead, she stayed where she was, looking longingly at the phone booth a few yards away.

'What are you doing out here, little girl?' She had not heard the car pull up, and she jumped with fright at the voice. The man, pushing his head through the open window, was white, balding and middle-aged. 'Looking for some fun?' he asked, as she stared at him in horror. She saw him opening the door, could smell the beer on his breath from where she was, and she made a dive for the phone booth, a fresh wave of shivers breaking over her. As she struggled with the door she remembered the many stories she had heard of people found murdered in this very park. She could see the other girls at school, remember their awed, whispered conversations about what had been done to the bodies. 'God help me, please don't let them whisper about me!' she prayed, the fear still clamouring in her, despite the fact that the car had driven off.

Her trembling fingers dialled the three nines as she prayed, and it seemed an endless time before a voice answered on the other end. Her voice shook so much, it took a long time to make herself understood, her throat clogging with fear and tears. But finally she had finished and stood huddled in the booth, shivering as much from reaction as from cold. She wondered if they would kill her straight away, or if they would torture her first like her father said. The tears flowed on, aching in her throat, the only warmth on her whole body. 'God, don't let them kill me!' she whispered. 'I didn't do anything. It wasn't my fault. I'm sorry I don't go to church but he wouldn't let me. Please, please don't let them kill me!'

She tried to banish her fear, fear of the white world juggling with the horrible image of that swollen exposed lump. 'I don't want to die,' she moaned, teeth chattering. 'Please don't let me die. I want to go home to my auntie.' She was immersed in her fear, huddled and shaking with the horror she had left and the one her imagination conjured up. The police car stopped unnoticed, and she froze, almost hysterical with fear, when the man and woman stood in front of her. She wished she had somewhere to run.

Instead she followed them into the car, tense and suspicious about their kindness, yet glad for the warmth that seeped into her.

From then on everything became a blur, her mind too dazed to take it in. She was in a small, windowless, grey room, and all she could feel was thankful it was so hot. The bright light from the naked bulb hurt her eyes, but she did not care, was past caring. She felt disoriented, bewildered by the constant jangle of endlessly ringing phones, the muted sounds of garbled voices seeming to come from all around.

Five

It was nearly time for the annual outing and the usual quiet discipline in the classroom had been replaced by high-spirited anticipation. Excitement bubbled over in a babble of confused sound as everyone tried to talk at once, vying with their neighbours to be heard above the din. For once the teacher was indulgent, seeming not to notice the noise, and she bent over the list of those going on the outing with the class monitor. Hyacinth shifted under the noonday sun, content to let the sounds swirl around her. The heat and the smell of warm grass tickled her nose, making her feel comfortable and belonging. She was really looking forward to this trip. They were going to Castleton Gardens this year, and her air of unconcern masked the fact that her mood mirrored the excitement of her classmates. She had never been to Castleton before, but she had heard so much about it. She could remember Florence boasting when her class had gone. Remembered how she had masked her envy with disbelief when the other girl had told her about the stream with stones so big that four children could sit on them, about seeing a crocodile lying in the sun, and the comb and brush tree that grew real brushes. Soon she would see them for herself, and then she, not Florence, would be the envy of the yard.

What a pity Cynthia had gone away, she thought suddenly. It would have been nice to see her face. After all, Cynthia was always boasting, but she had not been to Castleton either. She wondered where Cynthia had gone, when she'd be back. Suddenly, the sun was burning hot, uncomfortable, intruding on her peace. Hyacinth shifted unhappily, the strident voices intrusive now, threatening. She felt trapped, anticipation draining, leaving undefinable fear. The clear tone of the school bell cut across her growing apprehension, dragging her away from the oppressive heat. She came awake slowly, becoming conscious of the far-off sound of children's voices at play. She could hear the uneven sound of her breathing, the remnants of panic in the rapid beating of her heart, and for once she was glad of the safe reality of warm grass under her, and the lazy sounds of an English summer day. She lay unmoving for a moment, forcing the uneasiness back to its place in the recesses of her mind, preparing herself for the afternoon ahead, waiting for the second bell.

Sitting up reluctantly, she automatically glanced at the cheap plastic watch on her wrist, and could not prevent a quick stab of pleasure in ownership as she did so. She had bought it herself with her very own money, and she guarded it jealously. Hyacinth had never had pocket-money before, and she loved the feel of the coins in her palm; the knowledge that it all belonged to her. It made her feel important to own money, to be able to go to the shop and select what she wanted. It was nice to count out the coins from her little leather purse, to check her change before putting it safely in the snug pocket and clicking the lock shut, feeling satisfaction even in the noise it made.

The sound of the second bell had her scrambling to her feet. It wouldn't do to be late from lunch. She had physics next and the teacher always liked to start on time. Hyacinth hurried across the large sloping playing field towards the modern, glass-fronted school buildings. She liked this new school. It had three large, grass playing fields, with the grey stone playground, so similar to the one where she had spent those first miserable years, reserved for wet and windy days. Here the spite and name-calling was reserved for the Indians and even the teachers seemed friendlier towards her.

66

Only two hours until the school day was over. Hyacinth used the fleeting thought to glance at her watch again as she reached the classroom door. She wished school would last forever, that her secret wish to go to a boarding school could come true. She could have so much fun at boarding school, just like the girls in the stories which she read so avidly every week. Not that she was complaining. Her life since leaving her father's house had been a good one. The only bad thing was the reception home where they had taken her that night, and where she still lived seven months later despite earlier assurances that it would only be for a few weeks.

The reception centre was some miles outside the city, far enough away from her father for her to feel safe. The school she now attended had been chosen for similar reasons. At first she had liked the centre well enough, feeling relief from the continuous tension in her father's house. Even the lack of privacy, the sleeping in a dormitory with several strange white girls, had not bothered her too much. When she had first arrived there in the dead of night, the darkness and silence of the countryside unnerving after the constant traffic buzz of the city, she had been on tenterhooks in case her father's words about white people turned out to be true. Her teeth were almost chattering when the big red-faced woman who had come to the door frog-marched her to a small bathroom and demanded that she strip. She had been so relieved when the woman had made no move to hurt her, that she hardly noticed the other eyeing the bruises and scars on her body while she took a bath. Later, relief and weariness had sent her to sleep in the strange but clean-smelling bed.

By the end of the second week, relief had given way to another familiar tension. It was like being back at her old school again, except now she came home to it. Not even the satisfaction of pocket-money and the fact of having only one chore could compensate for that. With her growing uneasiness, the nightmare of her father's house now came to stalk her sleeping hours, mingling and interweaving with her jumbled, bitter memories of fiercely burning fires and screaming children. She felt alien among the white people, alien in the world of her dreams. Only the school hours offered some respite. There she was left alone, and her blackness hardly mattered. But at the home she hated everything.

The way her bath was always supervised, leaving her feeling naked and ashamed in her blackness, as one of the large red-faced women watched her with unblinking eyes. She knew everyone whispered about her hair, how grey and straw-like it was. It was not her fault that she could not find a big enough comb, that there was no oil to rub into her scalp. She was afraid to tell them that twice a week was too often to wash her hair, afraid they would call her dirty and blame it on her blackness.

Often she would think of Jamaica. Her hair had been nice then, long and soft to the touch. She would have thrown that at the taunting children but, once again, fear and shame at their response kept her silent. It was awful being different, and she hated the way people in the village near the home would nudge each other and stare when she passed. Only the knowledge of the evil she had escaped gave her any consolation, and her longing to return to Jamaica became a passionate force. That was where she belonged. There her colour didn't matter, for everyone else was the same. She would not have to be afraid of people at school finding out where she lived, Aunt Joyce would have welcomed them all. Not even the new clothes and warm bed at the reception centre could block out the dawning understanding that she was living in a charity home.

It was in the New Year that the house supervisor came to her, disturbing her as she sat on her bed, attempting to concentrate on her homework in spite of the noise of children at play. Hyacinth stiffened when the shadow fell across her, heart sinking when she looked up quickly and saw who it was. Mr Cluft had never hidden his dislike of her, often referring to her openly as 'nigger' and 'wog'.

'Yes sir,' she answered politely, eyeing him warily, when he called her name.

He told her there was someone to see her in his office, and Hyacinth felt sudden apprehension tingling down her spine. Was it the police again? Someone else? It was so many months now, surely they had asked her all the questions already? They frightened her, those official people. She hated the way they wrote down everything she said. She always felt they looked at her with suspicion and dislike . . . Yet they had stopped coming so long ago, and it was so late in the evening now.

Hyacinth climbed reluctantly off the bed, dragging her feet as she followed the supervisor to his room. Maybe it's him! The thought came abruptly, bringing her to a sudden halt, causing Mr Cluft to swing round with impatience, as he glanced back to see if she was still there. 'Hurry along, girl,' he said, an edge to his voice. 'Some of us have better things to do than wait around for you.'

She would have liked to refuse. But the man was waiting impatiently and she did not have the nerve to try and explain. She could feel the old horror returning, coming out of the shadows of her dream, causing her body to shake, and the sweat of fear to form on her forehead. She had never told them what he had done, but sometimes she fancied that they knew, could see the disgust written plainly in their faces. She wondered if Mr Cluft realised, could see the marks of her father's lust. Was it dislike that made him bring her father here?

'He can't do anything here,' she told herself nervously. 'They have to stop him if he tries.' Yet the words did not ring true, and the shaking got worse, the nearer to the door she came.

The man who got up when she entered the room was white, his hair a contrasting shock of grey. Relief made Hyacinth stumble, weakness flooding into her as the tension ebbed. Yet it was soon back. This man had the same unblinking stare, the same intimidating air that was so much a part of her father. She told herself he was white, that they were different from black people. At the same time she fancied she saw dislike, the same dislike that Mr Cluft and the other staff had for her.

'They don't like neaga here.' Her father's words came unbidden and unwelcome to her ears. She would have liked to blot them out, but in her heart she knew the truth of it. She had been in England over four years and always she had seen it and now, at the reception centre, she was forced to live with it. 'All these white people trying so hard to hide their hate,' she thought sadly. 'Yet they could kill you because you are different from them.' She always had to remind herself that they had not hurt her yet. Of course, they let her know she was not wanted, did not belong, but at least they were not violent like black people.

'Hyacinth . . . It is Hyacinth, isn't it?'

Hyacinth looked up startled, the man's voice unexpectedly gentle, as she stood awkwardly in the middle of the room.

'Why don't you take a seat?' he suggested, indicating the chair opposite the desk behind which he sat, as his big hands gathered the papers on the desk and shuffled them expertly into a pile.

She moved reluctantly and perched cautiously on the edge of the hard, high-backed chair.

'I'm Peter Adams from social services,' he said, holding out a hand.

Hyacinth nodded warily, putting her hand nervously in his, snatching it back almost immediately, and gripping it with the other in her lap. He seemed not to notice. 'I would like to ask you a few questions,' he said briskly, and she braced herself for what was to come. She could feel the familiar fluttering of fear in her stomach. Supposing he knew, supposing he had guessed what her father did?

'How many 'O' levels are you taking? Nine, isn't it?'

She looked up startled, not sure she had heard him right. No one ever asked her about school — not the police, not the other people who had come from social services, not her social worker, not even the staff at the reception home. She wondered what this man was up to, what he wanted. Her tension and unhappiness increased as the silence stretched on.

'Do you enjoy school?'

'Yes.'

He looked as if he expected more, and she cast around in her mind for something else to tell him. Found nothing. Gave up.

'No problems, no feeling of strangeness in a new school?' he persisted.

'I feel strange everywhere in this country, so it don't make any difference.' The words were out before she could stop them, pushing past the polite denial that she usually had ready for this question. He looked taken aback, unguarded annoyance flashing briefly in his eyes, picked up instantly by her frightened, searching gaze.

'I'm sorry,' she said quickly, penitently.

'If that is how you feel there is nothing wrong in saying it,' he said reassuringly. But she knew he was lying; that he was angry at her honesty.

'Did you find it easy to study at home?' he asked now, starting on a different tack.

Hyacinth was not fooled by the casualness of the question. It was so much like the ones she had been used to. The 'Did you find

70

it easy to live with your father? Did you resent your stepmother?' questions of those early months. 'No,' she said guardedly, not intending to make the same mistake again.

'Why was that?'

'I had other things to do.' She sensed his dissatisfaction with her answers, sensed it and was suspicious. After all, why should it matter if it was difficult to study at home? Why did he want to know about her schoolwork?

'You are not being very cooperative, are you?'

A cold sick lump formed in her stomach at the impatient question, sat heavily in her. She felt desperate, cornered. What could she say? If she told him the truth, he would not like it. Whatever she did he would be angry, she thought desperately, the trapped feeling growing. She wished he would just go and leave her in peace.

'I *am* trying to cooperate,' she said finally, knowing she sounded lame, yet not knowing what else to say.

'Do you like the countryside?' he asked, changing tack again.

'Yes, it's nice,' she responded, voice over-bright in an effort to convince him of her cooperation.

'Did you live in the countryside in Jamaica?'

She stiffened, wondered what he was trying to find out now.

'I lived in Kingston with my aunt.'

'Really?' he asked, genuine interest in his voice for the first time. 'I've been to Kingston once or twice,' he continued, adding, 'Which part of the city did you live in?'

Hyacinth looked at him in amazement, excitement building despite herself. Questions tumbled through her mind, lingered on her tongue. Was it as hot as she remembered? Did the iceman still come round with his cart? Had he tasted snow-cone, fudge, gizada? They piled through her mind, popping in and mixing in an excited jumble, but no words formed. 'He would look down at me if he knew where I lived,' she thought resentfully. 'He would probably tell the staff and make them treat me worse.'

'I lived in a big house in Mona . . . near the university.' The lie was out before she could stop it, or fully realised she intended it.

'Is that so?'

'He don't believe me,' she thought angrily as he smiled patronisingly at her.

'Black people live in nice houses in Jamaica,' she was stung to retort. 'They live there and have nice cars and good jobs.'

'I believe you,' he said mildly. And she knew he did not. She wanted to convince him, to wipe the smug look from his face, but already she had said too much, already he must think her rude.

'Were you angry about coming to England?' The bland question cut across her thoughts, throwing her into confusion.

'Yes. No,' she amended quickly.

He seemed not to notice the slip as he pressed on. 'I suppose you must have missed your aunt a lot?'

Hyacinth swallowed hard, as a lump suddenly formed in her throat. What did he know about Aunt Joyce? Who had told him? No wonder he had not believed her when she told him where she had lived. She glanced furtively at him, eyes quickly averted when they met his, her fingers curled with shame and resentment.

'Why are you afraid of me, Hyacinth?'

She darted a glance at the bland face, the insincere smile still there, and resentment nearly bubbled over out of control. What right had he to come here, to question her like this?

'You don't like black people!' she burst out. 'None of you do. You hate us. You hate me.'

The man looked slightly put out, and there was an edge to his voice. 'Why should I hate you?'

Hyacinth pressed her lips together, horrified at saying so much. She could feel tears clogging her throat and she struggled to stop them falling. This man knew so much about her, even more than her social workers who had known her for over a year. She wanted to ask him what he wanted, but instead she sat there feeling afraid, wondering what his motive was.

She was moving! Hyacinth heard the news with mingled joy and disbelief. She had wanted to move for such a long time. Already she had been at the centre for over a year. Other children had come and gone, but there was never anywhere suitable for her. She often wished she had the courage to ask to see one of the places they thought so unsuitable. Anything would have been better than staying where she was. If only they knew how much she had grown to hate the reception centre. Littlethorpe, the home she was moving to, sounded ideal, even though it was further out in the countryside than the reception centre. Any apprehension she might feel was buried deep. There was no one to talk to about it anyway. They could never understand how it felt to stand exposed and naked in her blackness, frightened by the hostile stares always turned on her.

The large rambling house her social worker took her to looked dusty and neglected, the red brick walls chipped and crumbling, the pale, watery afternoon sun exposing all the weaknesses and highlighting the dingy, run-down appearance. Hyacinth's heart had sunk as she watched the place approaching, knowing with certainty that that was where she was going. She wished with all her might that they would drive straight past. This place looked condemned and dilapidated. For a fleeting moment she wondered if it could possibly be better than the modern reception centre she had just left.

The interior lived up to the promise of the outside. It had an air of dirt about it, a dinginess that clung to the worn and faded carpet, the discoloured wallpaper and the musty-smelling, ageing furniture. Hyacinth stood in the middle of the large hallway, feeling strange and alone, wishing she had never agreed to come. She wished that she had the courage to tell her social worker just how she felt, but the thought of returning to the reception centre after leaving so triumphantly was more than she could bear. She felt misery weigh on her, longing for somewhere else to go, that she could somehow return to Jamaica. She was glad when her social worker went to search for the woman who ran the home.

The woman her social worker came back with was fat and greasy, eyes small blue chips in her long, heavy face.

'I'm Auntie Susan,' she said coldly. 'My husband, Uncle Alan, and myself are the house-parents here.'

Hyacinth nodded, not quite sure how she should respond to that. She wondered if she was expected to call the woman 'Auntie'. She could sense the woman's dislike, and it made her feel alone and desperate. It would be like this everywhere, all of them being polite — hating you, but hiding it. A sudden longing to be with black people surged within her, mingled with her usual sense of shame and guilt about her colour.

Hyacinth hated being the new girl at the home. The other children did not like her and it was like the nightmare of coming to

England all over again. She felt bitter at the way the staff ignored her suffering, trapped and desperate as she became the butt of jokes and cruelties, both within Littlethorpe and among the children from the surrounding homes. Going to school was liberation, but her feet dragged in the evenings in much the same way as they had done going home to the house of her father. She would have to steel herself for the taunts and jeers, the vicious pokes in her back, the slyly extended foot that tripped her when she was least aware. Most nights found her shaking and tearful as she crawled wretchedly into her bed. She often wished that she had nice hair, that her skin was lighter. She was sure they would not pick on her then. The more she suffered, the more she clung to thoughts of Jamaica, sinking further into her world of dreams, where she was never older than ten, never had to face the unpleasant reality that was England. It was only in the nightmares that her father came, the bulge exposed and menacing eyes spitting and burning with evil fire. But waking always brought reality, brought bitterness at the knowledge of her blackness, her ugliness a shameful weight that hung her head and bowed her shoulders. Try as she might she could not block out the other children's taunts, or even deny the truth of their words.

There was one girl in particular whom she watched with wary eyes. Sylvia Bell was a big, stocky girl, a few months younger than Hyacinth. She had often heard the other children whisper among themselves about the bad things she did with girls, and she kept out of her way as best she could. Sylvia reminded her of Margaret White and the humiliation she had heaped on her. She had no illusion that she could fight the bigger girl. Her fight with Margaret had been a fluke and the thought of getting into a fight with Sylvia left her shaking with fear.

One day, coming in from school, tired and buffeted by the wind, they met. Hyacinth stiffened when Sylvia appeared and moved to block her way up the stairs. The gleam of anticipation in the girl's eyes told Hyacinth that she had been waiting for her, and the familiar desperation seemed to swamp her. She was miserable and hungry, unable to cope with the other girl's taunts. She prayed that she would let her pass.

'You better say excuse me, liver lip, or you're not going anywhere,' the white girl said aggressively, as Hyacinth stood uncertainly at the bottom of the stairs. She felt unhappy and embarrassed about the whole situation, wanting only to be left alone.

'Can you excuse me, please,' she asked humbly.

Sylvia threw her head back, roaring with laughter. 'Can you excuse me, please,' she mimicked.

Hyacinth heard Auntie Susan's door open, close again with a definite click, and tears of self-pity rushed to her eyes. A sudden kick on her shin made her flinch, and she stepped hastily backwards, mind spiralling back to the nightmare days of her first school years in Britain. She could almost hear them shouting 'Kill the wog!' and her stomach churned sickeningly with fear of remembered pain. Panic welled up inside her. Sylvia's face looked evil and threatening, looming over her wickedly. She could not face another beating, could not go back to those days, not after so many years had passed. She had to do something, had to stop the panic spiralling up inside, and suddenly she dived at the other's leering face, wanting to tear it out of her way. She wanted, needed to escape to the safety of the waiting dormitory. Her fingers curled and sank into the pink cheek while her foot kicked viciously at the pale shin. She hated these white people, feared them, envied them, and the three emotions merged into a frustrated burst of feeling. At that moment she wanted to tear the girl apart, rob her of that skin that was so much a badge of acceptance.

Sylvia screamed, scrambling away from the sudden attack, sprawling down the stairs as her legs got tangled up and buckled under the unexpected attack. Hyacinth wasted no time scrambling on top of her, pounding at her, banging her head, trying to destroy her and the torment that she caused.

'Let Sylvia go this minute!' The woman's voice was like cold water trickling down her spine, seeping into her mind with the knowledge of what she had been doing, sobering her. Hyacinth's fist unclenched reluctantly, fingers slowly loosening their hold on the other girl's dress. Fear and alarm were rapidly replacing the satisfaction of pounding out her frustration on the girl's defeated head. She knew the woman would blame her for the fight, heard it in the impatience of the voice, felt the long knowledge of her hate.

'I want to talk to you in my room,' Auntie Susan said, as Sylvia struggled groggily to her feet. 'No, not you, Sylvia. I want to talk to Hyacinth.'

Hyacinth's heart sank; the woman blamed *her* for what had happened. Bitterness welled up inside her as she remembered the door opening, and the finality of rejection as it clicked shut, leaving her to her fate. It would have been different if Sylvia had beaten her up, she was convinced of this. They were all the same, these white people, they would always stick together against black people.

'I will not allow you to come here and establish jungle law!'

Hyacinth stiffened, sick with shame, hating the way the woman always lumped her in with other blacks. She knew she was different from other black people, even if she did look like them. She was not violent. But how could she tell this hard-eyed woman? How could she explain her fear? It was not her fault Sylvia had caused her to lose her temper. She knew it was wrong, that nothing the girl did would excuse her in the woman's eyes. But what else could she have done? She would have liked to have interrupted Auntie Susan, told her how she felt. Instead she hung her head, shame welling inside her, feeling small and disgusting.

'Having you here is one thing,' the woman was saying now, 'I had no choice about that. But one more incident like this evening and you are out. Do you hear me? Out!'

Hyacinth flinched, bitterness turning to panic, her tenuous hold on security slipping from under her feet, the nightmare of homelessness rapidly turning into reality. What would she do if Auntie Susan turned her out? Memories of the night she had left her father's house swam into her mind. The cold, the loneliness; the fat man in the car. No, she could not let that happen, she just could not. At the same time the unfairness of the situation bore down on her. She wanted to scream the truth at the woman, fear and anger mingling, warring inside her. She had to struggle to keep her mouth shut.

'Go and apologise to Sylvia, and let's have no more of this kind of behaviour from you,' Auntie Susan said finally, dismissively.

Hyacinth's head shot up, and she had to bite back the bitter words that threatened to spill over. The woman knew the fight had not been her fault, yet she was forcing her to apologise to the other girl. She felt tears clogging up her throat, anger making her head hurt. She wished she could refuse, could tell the woman she would not do it, but the memory of that terrible night was still with her, and she bowed her head in defeat.

'It's always the same,' she thought bitterly, 'just because I am black. I have to take the blame for everything. I'll never be treated same as them.' It was humiliating to have to apologise to her tormentor, and she wondered what the other girl would do once she found out that she had been blamed. She could imagine how it would spread around the three cottages of the home. Everybody would pick on her now. They would know that she would be held responsible for anything that happened, and she knew she would be too afraid of being kicked out of the home to fight back.

As it happened, the fight with Sylvia stopped the teasing. Now the others watched her warily, avoiding her as much as they could. Hyacinth was glad of this. She knew they still talked about her behind her back, but that was something she could live with. Even the unbelonging, the unwanted feeling was bearable, for at least they allowed her peace. 'One day I will have friends again,' she vowed often to herself. 'One day I will be back where I belong.' Jamaica was all she ever wanted, and she still visited it in her dreams, still treasured her aunt and confided in her friends. If the dreams were not always free from fear, she censored them, dismissed the unpleasant parts to the nightmares from which they had escaped. Yet for all that, the dreams were comforting in their unchanging state: security in an uncertain world.

At the same time there was an emptiness about her life, in her half-real world. Often she would lie awake in the silence of the night, perfectly still, the combined breathing of the other five girls in the room underlining her isolation. She would lie there staring into the impenetrable darkness, silent tears trickling from the corners of her eyes. She would have given anything for someone to talk to, someone to confide in.

By the time she reached sixteen the feeling that something was missing from her life had become an obsession. She often heard the other girls whispering among themselves, giggling with excitement. Often she would pretend to read a book, sitting in her corner, quiet and withdrawn, while thrilling to stories of what they did with boys. Yet always for her the image of her father would intrude, loom big and threatening above her; sick reality in the lump, exposed and obscenely menacing. The memory made her feel dirty, and she often thought the other children guessed. And still the emptiness grew inside her, yawned wide and open in her life. Now her night dreams left her strangely dissatisfied, peopled as they were with shadowy figures and flickering lights like fires. Now she no longer clung to the dreams as day broke, instead pushing them furtively to the back of her mind like something to be ashamed of. Even at school she would often catch herself staring absently through the window, wishing something new and exciting would happen to her today.

In this mood she discovered romance, found it between the pages of a stack of old Mills and Boon books that Auntie Susan had been about to throw away. Hyacinth loved the stories from the start, reading them from cover to cover, finding it hard to put them down, to concentrate on anything else. Now her lonely nights were peopled with tall, dark, handsome strangers, Spanish caballeros with warm brown eyes, romantic and intense Frenchmen. Sometimes in her secret fantasies she would be swept off her feet by a rich, passionate stranger and taken to live in his wild, remote castle. Always her hair would be blonde and flowing, her skin pale and white. Even at school she would daydream, ignoring the way her classmates nudged each other, pointed and sniggered, deaf to their crude comments and knowing looks.

She knew that many of the girls at school and at the home had boyfriends, and sometimes she envied them, envied the casualness with which they went to discos and youth clubs. She would never dare to go to one of the discos around Littlethorpe, conscious as she was of her colour, her strangeness. She could imagine them laughing at her, poking fun at her awkwardness, making rude comments about her skinny body and large bottom. The more she saw other girls dressed up, the more she envied them and wished she had been anything but black. They could never understand what it was like, how much she hated her brittle hair, the thickness of her lips. How could they understand what it was to be born like her? she often thought with bitterness. It wasn't fair. She had never done anything to deserve it. But she knew that no amount of anger and bitterness would change things. She envied the casual way the white children would cut their hair, secure in the knowledge that it would quickly grow again. Try as she might, her hair refused to grow, remaining stubbornly short and ugly; and she struggled to comb through the brittle dryness, afraid to use hair oil in case they thought her primitive. She always felt they were judging her, finding her wanting. And every time she felt inadequate, she would bury herself in another involved romantic plot, finding temporary relief as she had done for many years in a make-believe world.

Six

Hyacinth stared at the thin yellow strip of paper in stunned surprise, telling herself it could not be true. She couldn't have failed, not six out of nine. It couldn't be true. She felt bewildered, unable to grasp the implication of such failure. There had to be a mistake, something had to be wrong. How else could she fail six subjects out of nine? 'What am I going to do?' she asked herself desperately. She had to get that education. She just had to. She knew that Auntie Susan would insist she went to work now. That it would spell the end of her dreams.

'I'll go to college!' The idea hit her as she walked slowly along the dirt road behind the three cottage homes. A sudden surge of hope brought excitement bubbling up inside her. Thoughts of Auntie Susan intruded, and she pushed them away impatiently. 'Whatever happens, I have to get that education,' she vowed, and inside she knew it would mean a confrontation with the woman. One thing she knew: early tomorrow morning, she was going to find out how to apply to go to college, and somehow she was going to get there.

'You're going to do what?' Auntie Susan's pursed her lips as she looked at Hyacinth in disbelief. Hyacinth felt sick with nerve.

'I'm going to college to do my 'O' levels again,' she forced out, bracing herself for the scornful reply.

'You must be joking!' Auntie Susan exploded, anger and

contempt in her face.

Hyacinth lowered her eyes, bracing herself. She had expected this reaction, but it was no easier to bear.

'I am going to college,' she repeated stubbornly, toes curling in her shoes.

'What college will take you?' the woman sneered. 'Can't you blacks see there isn't any place for you in education? You had your chance and failed. Why don't you give up and stop wasting everybody's time?'

'Keene Fields have offered me a place to do the one-year 'O' level revision course,' Hyacinth mumbled, shifting uncomfortably under the hostile blue gaze.

The woman looked taken aback, but soon recovered herself. 'They did, did they?' she asked frostily. 'And I suppose they just wrote to you out of the blue and asked you to come.'

'I took their entrance exam three weeks ago. The results and the offer came today.'

'How dare you go behind my back and enrol!' the woman almost shouted. 'When did you become a staff member in this house, Miss Williams?'

Hyacinth stepped back, the sick feeling in her stomach increasing. Her father's voice came out of her nightmare, overlaid Auntie Susan's.

'You think you bad? A going to knock the rust off you.'

She closed her eyes tightly, pushing the image back. She was going to go to college, whatever the cost. The skin on her back stretched taut with remembered pain and expectation of punishment. 'I didn't go behind your back,' she almost pleaded, 'I didn't want to bother you with it until I knew if I had got the place. And now that I know, I thought I'd tell you before the enrolment next month.'

'Does your social worker know what you have been up to?' the woman asked now. 'I am sure if she found out she would be very angry with you.'

'She thinks it's a good idea,' Hyacinth answered, digging her nails into wet slippery palms.

The woman seemed put out, lost for words. 'I see,' she said coldly. 'And I suppose you are going to tell me next that she is going to pay for all this studying.'

'I was thinking of getting a part-time job,' Hyacinth responded, not daring to tell the woman that she had already done so, in case it upset her further.

'Well go and get your job and go to your college,' the woman snapped. 'But don't expect any help from me.'

Hyacinth breathed with relief. She had won. It was her first confrontation since leaving her father's house, and she had won. Her legs shook with reaction, but her heart sang with hope.

Hyacinth stood in the large hall, feeling strange and small, isolated by the noise of friendly chatter. Keene Fields was every bit as magical as she had expected. There were so many people, all wandering about looking important, books piled in their arms; and she couldn't wait to look like them. As she stood in line waiting to register, she couldn't help noticing how many black students there were. She supposed she ought to be glad that she no longer stood out, but she wasn't sure she liked the way they all bunched up together, and were so arrogant and rude to white people, nor the way they insisted on talking in that awful broken English so that the other students kept staring at them. They just seemed so ignorant, and she felt uncomfortable when several of them kept smiling encouragingly at her. She hoped none of them would approach her, hating the thought of being associated with them.

There were a number of Indian girls at the college and she found herself gravitating to them. She had got to like them when she was at school and had become quite friendly with several of them. They were nice people, Indians. They were not white, but they had long hair, and their noses were straight, their lips nice and thin. She liked their quietness and the way they stuck things out. The ones she knew had not been especially bright, but at least they kept going until they got what they wanted. She always made a point of ignoring the black students, lifting her nose high when they came close to her, feeling the need to establish herself as different in other people's minds.

There was one in particular whom she disliked. He was quite tall and she thought he would have looked quite nice if he wasn't so black. He had a nice mouth even though his nose was a little too big. He always made a point of blocking her way, grinning at her or giving her a wink every time he saw her pass. Hyacinth was always afraid he would try to talk to her, especially as he seemed to be one of the worst and loudest blacks. Halfway through the spring term her fears were realised. She was standing in the queue in the canteen one lunchtime, talking to one of her Indian friends, when she saw him approaching out of the corner of her eye. She prayed he would walk past, that he might not notice her, and her heart sank when he stopped right beside her.

'Hello,' he said cheerfully. 'I see you around college all the time. What are you studying?'

Hyacinth turned her head away, feeling awkward and embarrassed, willing him to go away. She knew that people were watching them, and she dreaded the thought that they might think she was like him.

'Aren't you going to answer me?' he persisted.

Hyacinth cast a furtive look at her friend, mouth stretching into a self-conscious smile as she saw the other girl watching her with speculation. Why didn't he go away? Why did he have to stand there showing her up? She wanted to walk away, but feared he would take out his crude spite on her friend, so she stayed, praying he would grow tired and leave.

'What's the matter with you? Cat get your tongue, or do you just prefer coolies to your own kind?' He was getting annoyed, and she felt her stomach muscles tense, all desire for food leaving her.

'What do you see in coolies, anyway?' the boy went on. 'They always smell of garlic and grease.'

Hyacinth heard the Indian girl beside her gasp, and desperation surged up inside her. Indians were so sensitive, they would never forgive her once this got out. She had to shut the boy up, stop him before he ruined things for her. Keene Fields would be so big and lonely without her Indian friends. 'Blacks are always out to ruin things for each other,' she thought bitterly, 'but I'm not going to let him get away with it this time.'

'Don't you have anything better to do with your time?' she asked angrily, nails biting into her palms.

The youth grinned irrepressibly, encouraged by her response. 'You shouldn't get annoyed 'cos a bloke fancy you,' he said, laughter in his voice.

'Well I don't fancy you,' she exploded, feeling resentful at his playfulness.

'Why not? Do you prefer coolies?'

Hyacinth looked up at the ceiling, feeling heat creep into her face, sure that the whole canteen was looking at her, laughing at her.

'Hey, tell me something,' the youth said now, giving Hyacinth a friendly nudge. 'Is it true the blokes have to play with it before they can . . . you know?'

The Indian girl shifted restlessly, and Hyacinth dared not look at her; she wanted to ask her if she was OK, but instead stood still, staring blindly in front of her.

'I'm going,' the Indian girl said stiffly. 'I'm not staying to listen to this.'

Someone close by mimicked the accented voice and Hyacinth stiffened, a vision of her first tortured school year flashing in front of her, bringing back memories of the circling crowd, the faces of hate and anger bearing down on her. The Indian girl's attempt to push past her brought her back to her present reality.

'Don't go,' she said desperately, putting out a restraining hand. 'Just ignore him.'

The girl looked at her with hostility. 'Are your people always like this?' she asked coldly.

Hyacinth's hand dropped to her side, allowing the girl to pass. Shame sat on her like a burden. It was so unfair that she should be mistaken for one of them, that she could not deny their common stock. She would have left straight after the Indian girl if the youth had not grabbed one end of the long grey scarf she always wore around her neck.

'Let the coolie go,' he said provocatively. 'Can't you see she don't want you?'

She gave him a withering look. 'I'll thank you not to call my friend a coolie,' she said frostily.

'And I suppose it's all right for them to call us niggers?'

'As that is what we are, yes . . . Well, not niggers, but negroes, certainly.'

'Is that how you really think!' He sounded surprised, angry, as if she had let him down somehow. Hyacinth resented that. How dare he make her feel like that!

'I'm not ashamed of what I am, even if the rest of you are,' she said defiantly. 'And anyway, colour don't matter, it's what the person inside is like that count.'

'Je—sus!' he said, dropping the end of her scarf as if it was poisoned. 'They really have you screwed up, don't they?'

Hyacinth looked at the youth in surprise. That was rich coming from him. If anyone was screwed up it was him. He certainly had a chip on his shoulder.

'I don't know what you're talking about,' she said in a carefully neutral voice.

'I bet you don't at that,' he answered in disgust. 'Girl, you really are backward.' He turned abruptly, walked away, and she watched him leave with satisfaction. It was just the thing to expect from blacks, she thought smugly, calling other people backward to hide their own inferiority. Well, thank God she was above such things.

The black students ignored her after the incident in the canteen, all of them giving her strange looks, whispering about her. Hyacinth was glad, thankful to have got them off her back. Fortunately the Indians had remained friendly. They told her they knew how things were, assured her that she was different. She was grateful to them, thankful for the politeness that made them so tactful. They made her feel included. True, they spent most of the time talking in their own language, and often she would hear her name laughingly mentioned, but she didn't mind that. It was nice to have a language of your own, and people just had to understand and be tolerant. She liked the Indians a lot; they were so studious, it forced her to do some work, spend less time on romantic novels, and she had no trouble passing her 'O' levels at the second attempt.

She was back on course now, 'O' levels safely past, 'A' levels going well, and Hyacinth felt relaxed and confident about her eventual goal. Another year and a half and she would be at university. She was content to let the time drift by, feeling nothing could cloud her horizon again. Even at night dreams got more infrequent, less necessary now that she was so close to realising her goal. Now, when they came, they were peopled with confused pictures, blurring the edges of her enjoyment with disturbing background images.

It was soon after the end of her first 'A' level term that Auntie Susan started dropping hints that she wanted Hyacinth to leave the home. At first Hyacinth ignored her, sidestepped the issue, until one day the woman confronted her as she got in from college.

'How much longer do we have to put up with you?' the woman asked bluntly, after calling Hyacinth into her sitting-room. 'You're seventeen and still here, when we need the place for someone else.'

The old familiar sickness invaded Hyacinth's stomach. She couldn't leave, where could she go? She had no illusion that the £6.50 she earned from her part-time job would pay rent somewhere and feed her as well. Thoughts tumbled around in her head, fuelled by her panic. She couldn't leave college, not now, not when things were going so well for her.

'I thought I didn't have to leave until I was eighteen,' she ventured tentatively, feeling her small security slipping from her, a big uncertain nothingness yawning in front of her.

The woman snorted. 'Who told you that?' she asked aggressively. Hyacinth felt ill. Wasn't it true? God! She had been so sure of that, had counted on it.

'I . . . I got that impression when my social worker told me that I was in care until I was eighteen,' she said now, a vision of working in a factory, an office, looming before her.

'You're under Section One,' the woman said nastily. 'You came into voluntary care, and now you are taking up space that is needed for urgent cases.'

Hyacinth swallowed hard. She knew the woman didn't care who needed the space, knew she only wanted to get rid of her. She could not think what to say, how to answer. 'I'll go and see my social worker,' she said finally, diffidently.

The woman's lips compressed. 'You do that, miss,' she said spitefully. 'But don't think that threat means much coming from the likes of you. This place was never intended as a boarding house for college students. You should have left here when you were sixteen.'

Hyacinth said nothing. It would be pointless trying to convince the woman that she had not intended to complain. Auntie Susan disliked her, and short of changing her colour there was nothing she could do about it.

It was inevitable that she should dream that night, escape to a Jamaica which seemed to be slipping away from her in her waking life. They had gone to visit Cynthia, Florence and she. Cynthia, who had returned from the country that very day. As usual, they sat in the shed behind the house, huddled together as they exchanged scary duppy stories in whispered voices. Hyacinth felt more and more nervous as the shadows grew longer, pressing closer to Florence, trying to hide her fear of the growing darkness. Only the knowledge of the street outside stopped her from taking her leave. She hoped Florence would be ready soon. The thought of walking through the heavy darkness, past the doorways clogged up with ignorant men, was more than she could face alone. At the back of her mind she knew he lurked in the shadows — Cynthia's father, so big and aggressive. They never mentioned him.

She was relieved when Florence finally made a move to go. The heat in the shed had become unbearable and she was choking in the stale air. She was quick to follow Florence, ignoring the pleading in Cynthia's brown eyes, the desperation she knew so well. They could not stay here, could not burn up in the other's fear. She kept close to Florence as the girl walked through the gate, the smell of wood smoke catching her throat, making her eyes smart. She hated that smell which always clung to this street, and she hurried to put some distance between it and herself. But the smell followed her, lingered in her nose . . . through the layers of sleep until she woke to the smell of burning leaves, and other autumn country smells.

'Your social worker left, dear.'

Hyacinth stared at the woman behind the long, white reception desk in dismay.

'Left!' she repeated blankly, feeling suddenly weak. 'When?'

'About two weeks now, ducks.'

Bile rose in her throat, had to be forced down. She had deliberately left college early, so that she could come to the impressive three-storey glass and concrete building that housed the social services department. Now her social worker had gone, and had not even told her she was going.

'What am I going to do?' she wailed desperately.

'Do?' The woman looked up from the pink garment she was

knitting with the speed of long practice. 'Why, see someone else, love,' she said kindly. Hyacinth felt a little surge of hope. But, would someone else see her? Would someone else know what to do?

'You aren't half in a state, love,' the woman said, resting her knitting on her lap and turning her full attention on Hyacinth. 'Go on, sit yourself down and I'll get someone out. One of the social workers will soon put you right.'

She was sitting nervously on one of the green easy chairs when her name was called out. Her throat ached from the effort of holding back the tears that clouded her vision and burned in the lining of her nose. The woman was slim with mousy hair and introduced herself as Celia Parks, Hyacinth's new social worker.

'I intended to get in touch with you before, but I'm afraid I got a little tied up,' she apologised.

'That's OK,' Hyacinth said automatically, trying to suppress the bitterness inside. She wondered if her old social worker would have treated her like that if she had been white, and if this one would not have got round to her sooner. She pushed the thought aside impatiently, concentrating on her present predicament instead. At the moment it didn't matter how the woman felt about her as long as she could help her.

When she had explained the problem, Celia Parks smiled reassuringly. 'You needn't worry on that score,' she said briskly. 'Whatever the house-mother says, you can stay at the home until you are eighteen, then we shall help you find somewhere to live and support you through your 'A' levels.' Hyacinth felt relief. That was exactly what she had not dared hope for. She wondered how Auntie Susan would take the news, how she would dare to tell her, but once again the woman stepped in.

'Look, I know Susan Irish can be difficult,' she now said. 'So if you want me to, I'll come up and have a word with her about the matter.'

Hyacinth nodded eagerly, feeling the last weight lift from her. 'I'll really study hard now,' she told herself in sudden optimism. 'I am really going to make all this worth while.'

It was a couple of weeks later that she came back from college early to find a black youth dressed in army uniform comfortably seated in Auntie Susan's sitting-room, the door thrown wide open. Hyacinth hid her surprise at seeing him, making no attempt to acknowledge him as she passed to get to the stairs. As far as she knew, Auntie Susan hated black people so his presence could only be business and she certainly did not want to know about it.

The youth turned out to be an ex-resident of the home who had left at sixteen some three years previously. Hyacinth had heard tales of Colin Matthews, heard the pride in Aunt Susan's voice when she spoke of him, and she was shocked and disappointed to find out that he was black. She hated him on sight, resented the way he fitted in so well, felt shame at the way he seemed to hang on to the white people, and envy that they allowed him to do it. It was so unfair, the way the white girls came to see him in droves. She hated the way Auntie Susan patted him on the head, the fondness with which she showed him off.

Colin Matthews took great delight in baiting Hyacinth, sensing her wariness and insecurity, playing on them. She hated the way he ran after the white girls, feeling more and more inferior as she saw them, big-busted and confident, pressing close to him in some secluded spot.

'You're too ugly for my use,' he often told her. 'I like long blonde hair, something I can run my fingers through.'

Hyacinth shrank into herself, telling herself she was glad, that he was like her father anyway, and it was good he had no time for her. Yet his words made her feel inadequate. She felt small when he ignored her, or poked fun at her hair and bottom. How could she compete with white girls? They were always passing through, lingering to get a glimpse of him, phoning constantly to invite him out. None of them seemed to mind that there were so many others. Hyacinth resented it, could not understand it. By her standards, he was uglier than her if that was possible, and yet he made her feel deformed.

'If only I could do something about my hair,' she often thought, distastefully fingering a coarse plait. Now she would look at the thin pink lips of the other girls at the home with envy. She took to pressing her lips together, trying to narrow the line, thinking that if Colin Matthews, whose lips were much thicker, could comment on them; everyone else must be doing so as well.

It was while she was feeling this new sensitivity that Hyacinth found herself in the Highfields area one day. She had generally avoided it since leaving her father's house, but the need to go there had become a growing obsession since Colin Matthews' arrival. She was not even sure why she wanted to go there, why she should feel this sudden need to mix with her own people after being at such pains to distance herself from them for so long. It was a few years since she had last walked the shabby streets, but still the poverty smells, the old familiar dread, returned to haunt her — the skipping heartbeat when a man loomed in the distance, the constant checking over her shoulder in case he had doubled back and was creeping on her from behind. They were like her father, the black men up here, aggressive and rude, dirty and smelling of drink.

It took her a while to realise that the place had changed since she lived there. But gradually the Indian smells invaded her consciousness, just as they had crept into the area and replaced the West Indian smells. She became aware of the lack of Jamaican accents with a sense of shock. They had been so much a part of the area. Now Eastern Caribbean people, sounding so much like her stepmother, had replaced them. The streets looked seedy and blighted as she wandered along, and there was something eerie about the silent rows of condemned and boarded-up houses, doors hanging off their hinges where vandals had forced their way in.

'I'll never end up here again,' she vowed fiercely, wrinkling her nose as the smell of dereliction assaulted her. How could her father have brought her from Jamaica to this? She had been happy with Aunt Joyce, happy, content and belonging. She hurried along, suddenly eager to get away from the decay, the disturbing familiar smells raked up by the heat of the summer day, and the hordes of flies buzzing round the foul-smelling bins.

The garish orange shopwindow was too bold to miss, standing out bright and startling against the drabness of the rest of the street: 'Cerema's Beauty Booth'. Hyacinth walked up to it, a half-formed idea in her mind. 'We specialise in turning ugly ducklings into swans,' read the bold promise underneath the shop name and, in smaller print, 'Specialists in Afro hair, cold and hot straightening'.

Hyacinth's heart raced at the vision it conjured up. Could she be beautiful? Would she dare? God, it would be so nice not to be ugly. Almost unthinkingly she pushed open the door, regretting it immediately as the action set up a clamour of bells, causing everyone inside to look up. She would have liked to retreat, to back out from under the battery of stares, but it was too late. A woman in a white overall was already coming towards her, and she knew how rude black people could be if you upset them.

Two hours later she left the salon feeling dazed and shocked, hardly able to believe the transformation had actually happened. 'You are quite a looker,' the hairdresser had said as she combed out the newly styled hair, and now the words echoed in her head. Hyacinth marvelled at the length of her hair, could not resist feeling the soft straightness between her fingers. She was glad she had chosen cold-straightening, disliking the way steam had risen in a cloud from a hot comb being applied to another customer's hair, the way the woman tensed and jerked as the comb slipped on her scalp. Her treatment had been painless, and it looked just as good. She could not resist looking in the shopwindows as she passed, slowing her step to enjoy the new picture she presented. She could hardly wait for them to see her at the home; and when they did, was gratified by the silence, the way their conversation tailed off as they noticed her. She might not have long hair, but at least it looked as nice as theirs now.

It was Colin Matthews' reaction that she liked most. He had not been there when she got in, but being seventeen, she was allowed to go to bed when she wanted and she was still in the children's sitting-room when he came in. Hyacinth's heart hammered with anticipation as she heard him come through the front door and she braced herself as he paused outside. She told herself that she had not been waiting for him, that the book she was reading was too good to put down even though she had read less than ten pages all night.

She had been sitting strategically, so as to be visible from the doorway, and he stopped short at the sight of her, disbelief written across his face.

'We—ell!' he said, after a long pause, the word drawn out on a long whistle. 'What a turn up.'

Hyacinth pretended indifference, feeling suddenly hot and shy. Now that she had achieved her objective she wasn't sure what to do; was not even sure it had been worth it. She sat still, eyes on the book, casting around desperately in her mind for something to say. All the smart things she had dreamt of saying to him fled, and she finally decided that she might just as well go to bed. Getting to her feet she made to walk past him.

'Not so fast, baby!' he said in a phoney American accent, the one she often heard him using to his many girlfriends.

Hyacinth stopped short, feeling suddenly nervous and afraid. Her heart was hammering and her eyes glanced down almost compulsively. Then her heart nearly stopped. 'He has a lump!' she thought in panic, suddenly swamped with remembered fear, legs shaking as she backed a step.

'Come and sit down and talk to me,' he said suggestively, holding out a hand to her.

Hyacinth stumbled backwards, the remembered nightmare, magnified by time, reaching out to close around her.

'N . . . no thank you,' she said hastily, rubbing sweaty palms against the seat of her jeans.

'What's the harm?' he coaxed. 'Girl, I never knew under the skin you had something there.' The nightmare had come back to life. As she backed away, she saw him bearing down on her, big and obscene, smelt the liquor on his breath. She could feel the scream bubbling up inside her, had to struggle to force it down, to swallow it.

'Hey, I was only joking, I didn't mean it.'

Hyacinth did not hear him, could only see him coming at her, hear Maureen's voice — 'You better watch your father,' her words jumbling with the others, the ones ringed with black ink in the middle of the abandoned book, 'Incest flourished where the roads were bad'. They spun round and round in her head, a jumbled mixture of terror and guilt.

'Hyacinth, are you all right?' The words sounded high-pitched, young and frightened, nothing like her father, bringing reality back, with the knowledge that Colin's lump had gone. 'It's all right,' he said hastily. 'I was only joking. There's no need to act so spooky.'

She crept round him, keeping wary, suspicious eyes on him as she edged towards the door, hardly daring to breathe as she slipped through it and scrambled hastily up the stairs. She could not stop shaking, even after she pulled her nightdress on and crawled into bed.

They were scrambling over the rocky slope, too hot to bother talking to each other. Hyacinth was very careful not to get her new white dress dirty. She could just imagine her aunt's fury if she found out where she had been.

'Hyacinth, hurry up noh man.'

Florence's impatient voice brought her attention to the fact that the other girl was well in front of her. The sun was hot on her back, the wind full of dust as she increased her pace. The late afternoon noises floated to her from the nearby shanty dwellings, the jukebox music making her feet itch to dance. Florence was waiting for her at the bottom of the slope, and Hyacinth could not suppress a feeling of smugness at her own neat appearance in the face of the other girl's ripped and faded dress. It was then that she noticed the large tear right in the centre of her own dress. She felt sick. How was she going to explain it? She felt a sense of irritation as the wind blew her long straightened hair against her face. What was the point of it, if it only got her in trouble?

'Come noh man!'

Florence's impatient voice interrupted her thoughts. 'I thought you wanted to go to Salter shop for fry fish.'

Hyacinth suppressed her worry, assuring her friend she would buy her the fish. She could not back out now. The dress was already torn and there was nothing she could do about it. Yet the apprehension persisted, and suddenly she wished she could be like Florence, so unchanging and unconcerned, not like her and poor Cynthia. Despite her ugly neglected appearance, her coarse hair, Florence was better off than both of them, for she never had to worry about anything.

The smell of the fish, usually so appetising, turned her stomach, mingled with her fear, and sat heavily inside her. She wished with all her heart that she could turn back, that she had never decided to come. It would be so nice just to sit under the clammy cherry tree, to lie there and watch the birds flying lazily by, swooping and whirling in the cloudless sky. She could hear bottles clanking as the shopkeeper gathered them from the counter, the sound getting louder and louder, rattling in her ears. Turning back, she tried to ask Florence why they were so loud, but woke instead to the cheerful whistle of the milkman.

She lay there for a few moments, feeling shaken and disturbed by the jumbled, vivid dream. The incident of the night before forced itself into her consciousness, as she closed her eyes against the warm rays of the morning sun. God, she hated black men, she thought with revulsion, tears slipping from under her closed lids. Shame made her want to hide under the pillow, never to emerge again. How could she look at him again? They were all the same, all of them. If only she had not straightened her hair . . . if only she was not black. The thoughts tossed around in her head, feeding the bitterness she had lived with since leaving her father's house, caused by the knowledge that nothing she could do would change what she was.

She forced her mind away from it, thought instead of what the day would bring. It was Saturday, and today she was going with her social worker to look for a place to live. She would be eighteen in a few weeks' time, and she knew it was urgent that she find somewhere to live soon. Hyacinth had wanted to go to the Citizens' Advice Bureau and get a housing list for herself. She felt sure that she would have had no difficulty finding somewhere to live, especially as social services had undertaken to pay the rent. But her social worker had dissuaded her, pointing out that she would be able to get a better place through social services. In a way Hyacinth was looking forward to moving out of the home, to be able to get some privacy, look after herself. She was a little frightened about how she would manage, but told herself bracingly that it would be practice for university. As far as she could see, social services would take care of her; and if she was careful with her money, she could continue to save all that she earned in much the same way as she had been doing since going out to work, nearly two years before.

Seven

It was a drab, miserable place, its only advantage the fact that it was cheap. But what else could she do? There just wasn't enough time to find something else. Disappointment lay heavily on her, bending her under its weight. All the problems she had thought about had not prepared her for this.

'You can decorate it if you like,' the warden said encouragingly.

Hyacinth looked at the woman blankly, lost in her bitterness, only half-hearing the words. She kept her mouth clamped shut, throat aching with unshed tears.

'Oh yes, I could try to decorate it,' she thought cynically, looking around at the soiled grey walls and dirt-encrusted carpet. She wouldn't even know what paint to buy. Anyway, what would be the point? Why bother with a nice room in a house for ex-cons? How had she returned to this? her mind asked over and over again. Could they have guessed her secret? Maybe she should have just told them why she had left home. Maybe it was because she had hidden her guilt. She supposed in a way she deserved to be there. She should have been punished for what her father had tried.

'It's not all that bad, Hyacinth,' Celia Parks said coaxingly. 'It's only for a year and it really was the best we could do in the circumstances.'

Hyacinth looked at her in silent contempt. She should have known not to trust a white woman. They were all the same, all promises and smiles to her face, all scheming hatred and spite behind her back. The social worker dropped her eyes, shifted uncomfortably under the hostile stare.

'Once you have decorated it, it will really look quite nice,' she said hastily. 'And any money you spend will, of course, be refunded.'

Hyacinth said nothing, ignoring the two of them, pretending she did not feel their anticipation of her assent.

'Well?' her social worker asked finally, breaking the silence. Hyacinth bit hard on her bottom lip, trying to control the feeling of betrayal. It was hard to form the words, to condemn herself to this living hell. But finally she managed it.

'I'll come,' she said shortly, the words flat with reluctance.

Her social worker gave an audible sigh, and she felt blinded by sudden tears. She had really believed that Celia Parks would help her, had almost forgotten why she distrusted white people when dealing with the woman.

'They don't like neaga here,' her father's words echoed in her mind with fresh meaning, and she vowed she would never be caught again.

In no time at all it seemed she had moved into the hostel, clothes crammed into the broken-down wardrobe, a few personal possessions on the grey-looking dressing table with the cracked mirror. She had scrubbed the room from top to bottom, but it still felt dirty, looked grey and neglected. It was a warm September, but the place had a permanent chill, and she spent most of her time huddled over the small gas-fire for warmth.

Although the grant from social services paid both the rent and heating costs she increased her working hours, needing to be away from the depressing room as much as possible. She had opened a bank account on her social worker's advice, and she was able to deposit a full twelve pounds a week into savings. Hyacinth had no interests apart from Mills and Boon novels, and these she bought second-hand from one of the many specialist stalls in the market.

If anything, her loneliness had increased. She found that she missed the noise and bustle of the home, her new isolation intensified by the muted sound of voices that drifted through the floor from the common-room downstairs. She was too shy, too used to her own company to try mixing with the other tenants more than necessary; and after one of them mentioned casually that he had killed his sister she kept away from them entirely. She spent long hours in the college library, hanging around until it closed, and on other days she worked. Sunday was the worst day, empty hours stretching endlessly. The effort of lurking behind her door, ears straining for an empty space in which to dart to the kitchen or bathroom, get through cooking and washing, and scurry back to the safety of her own room without being seen, often proved too much for her, and she would avoid cooking altogether, either going without food or making do with chips. She took to walking around the large park nearby, daydreaming about what it would be like when she finally returned to Jamaica.

Soon she was walking everywhere. There was no need to hurry back to her lonely room, nothing to go back to. As the days grew colder, she watched the grass get greener, the leaves fall from the trees, and she dreaded the approaching winter, the long and lonely Christmas holidays which loomed so large on her horizon. As the shop-windows filled with cheerful decorations her isolation intensified. She felt detached from the Christmas frenzy. There would be no presents to expect this year, none to give. Hyacinth had never really enjoyed Christmas in England, but there had at least been something to look forward to. At her father's house it had spelt a respite from the constant beatings. At the home the presents had been practical and useful. But now there was nothing and the Christmas spirit passed her by. She had refused the hostel warden's invitation to join the other residents for Christmas. She was too wary of them to feel at ease in their company, and much as she would have liked the sense of belonging, she knew she would have hated every moment of being with them.

An oversized Christmas tree appeared in the common-room about ten days before Christmas. It was laden with decorations and presents, and its cheerful coloured lights seemed to wink mockingly at her as she passed. Hyacinth often caught herself thinking wistfully of the television and record-player in the common-room, wished she had the nerve to go down and use them. She would tell herself grimly that those things would be hers one day. She would never live like this again.

The sound of Christmas carols drifted up through the floorboards, replacing the usual rock'n'roll. It brought a wave of longing for Jamaica, and thoughts of dimly remembered happy Christmases. There was almost a religious air about the hostel now, a sense of anticipation as the days slipped by. Finally Hyacinth woke to the cheery sounds of Christmas greetings. She lay in the narrow bed, feeling isolated and unhappy. There was an appealing smell of roasting meat on the cold air, and she felt an unbearable wave of longing and homesickness. Tears of self-pity filled her eyes, spilt down her cheeks. She did not have the energy to move, to do anything but lie there, feeling unhappy, drifting in and out of sleep.

Hyacinth could feel her heart pound with excitement, feet itching to run to the gate. If she strained her ears, she could just make out the noise of the drums and the merry sounds of the flute. They were coming in this direction! They were going to pass right by the gate. She willed Aunt Joyce to hurry, not wanting to miss any of the procession. She wanted to be at the gate when they came into sight, wanted to feel her heartbeat mingle with the drumbeat and tapping feet. The music was coming nearer and she hopped about impatiently.

'Come on, Aunt Joyce,' she muttered under her breath. They were nearly there and still no sign of her aunt. 'Hurry, Aunt Joyce, hurry! Hurry! Hurry!' she whispered over and over. She could have shouted in relief when her aunt finally appeared, looking nice and cool in her peach church dress and matching hat. Now she could run to the gate, and if she hurried she would catch most of the dancers.

'Hyacinth, come and get the money, chile.'

Hyacinth paused in mid-stride, pretty pink dress swirling around her. She could have groaned aloud. She would surely miss the dancers now. 'John Cunoe, naw goh run weh,' Aunt Joyce chided when she saw Hyacinth's impatience.

Hyacinth did not answer, scooping up the money from her aunt's large palm, and turning to run to the gate. She leant over it, peering into the distance, trying to get a glimpse of the dancers in the distance. The music was getting louder, the pounding drums more insistent, but still there was no sign of a band, no dancers appearing along the wide, well-kept street. Hyacinth frowned, looking from one side to the other. How could that be? The music was so loud, it was everywhere. How could the band and dancers not be there? Yet search as she would, the street remained empty, drowsing in the mid-December sun.

'Where are the dancers?' she asked, turning to her aunt in bewilderment. Aunt Joyce's mouth moved, but now the music was so loud her words were swallowed up by the din. Hyacinth tried to shout above the rising sound, feeling alarmed as it became more strident, more discordant. She wanted to get away from it, from the sudden tinniness of the drums, the artificial whine of the electric guitar. Running back to Aunt Joyce she tried to get her attention, shaking her, pulling at her skirt. But the woman talked on, not even noticing the sound that made her so uncomfortable. She felt a stab of resentment, a sudden anger towards her aunt. Covering her ears she ran towards the house. Her Christmas was ruined now, so there was no need to stay. But the music followed her, beat at her, blotting everything out as she awoke to find the walls of the dingy room reverberating around her.

After Christmas the winter was more bearable. Hyacinth had become used to the cold and loneliness outside college. She had no fears about passing her exams. She knew her work was good, having little else to do with her time apart from work. But even she noticed the approaching spring. Now, as she walked through the park, or down the road to town, there was no need to huddle so far into her duffle coat. She enjoyed the cheerful sound of bird song bringing her awake to warmer days, the cool fresh sounds on the morning air as she walked briskly across the dew-wet grass, or strolled along the uneven pavement. Everything seemed sharper this year, full of hope, and she was aware that only months lay between her and the exams that would move her on, especially chemistry, the subject she had chosen as the one she would study.

She often thought of the conditional university place offer that lay carefully hidden under her clothes in her drawer, and hugged the knowledge to herself. It was her secret, and often eager impatience would surge up inside her when she thought of the time that still lay in front of her. And so spring slipped slyly into summer, bringing hot dry days like the year before, which plastered the thin cotton dress to her back and sharpened her longing to be back at home. She moved her bed to the long, narrow window of her room so that the first rays of the sun could seek her out, to warm her awake on weekdays, and heat her daydreams on Sundays.

One Sunday she lay in bed, deliberately allowing her mind to wander until daydream was swallowed up by sleeping dream. She was in the garden of the big new house where she and her aunt now lived in the world of her dreams, lying on her back in the shade of the tall, clammy cherry trees. Hyacinth strained her ears, trying to make out the sound of approaching footsteps. Florence and Cynthia were going to call for her, and she wanted to be there when they arrived. She didn't want to go to Cynthia's house. She would much rather stay where she was, listening to the rustling leaves and the whirling sound of the doctor bird as it sipped nectar from the deep pink hibiscus flowers. But she knew she had to go. Cynthia was her friend, and Florence would be there as well, and besides, she would be able to show them what she had hidden in her drawer before they went.

The sound of footsteps crunching on the gravel path had her scrambling to her feet, running eagerly to meet her friends. Then she was herding them up to her little pink and blue room, eager to share her secret. Hyacinth felt her heart swell with pride at her friends' admiring glance.

'Just wait till they see what I have to show them,' she thought as she went eagerly to the grey dressing table.

It was gone! The slip of yellow paper she had pinned her hopes on was gone! Behind her, Florence and Cynthia giggled, and she turned in time to see Cynthia set a lighted match to it, a gleam of malice in her sad eyes. Anger and panic rose in her, and she lunged at the other girl, but Cynthia skipped out of the way, holding aloft the burning paper. All she could do was watch impotently as the flames spread, crept down to the girl's hand, engulfed it. Cynthia was burning! Hyacinth heard Florence scream, stood with frozen horror, watching, unable to move. Then everything was burning and she and Florence had somehow stumbled out.

They had left Cynthia! Left her burning! She felt sick at the thought, saw the face contorted in pain, the hands clawing ineffectually at the window-pane. Cynthia was burning and they had left her there. She would have liked to run back, to help, but her paper was burnt already. She would never get away now. She could hear people running about behind her, shouting, screaming and accusing. The heat was unbearable, reaching out for her, forcing her to stumble back, to struggle up through the layers of sleep, shaking and bathed in sweat.

Her first reaction was to scramble out of bed, pull out the drawer, panic clawing at her. It was still there! It was there, neatly folded, right where she had left it, and in her relief she allowed the dream to slip away.

The days had become so hot that Hyacinth took to revising in the park, often dozing in the sun. She awoke one day to the knowledge that she was being watched. Hyacinth stiffened, feeling embarrassed, wondering if her mouth had been slack, if she had been snoring. She shifted uncomfortably, feeling exposed. She couldn't resist glancing round to see who had been watching her. Her eyes collided with a man's, and shifted away quickly, ducking down into the safety of her book. But he continued to watch her, and she looked up again, furtively. This time he smiled, causing a lurch of fear inside her. He was black, older than her, and although he was well-dressed, the fact of his presence brought the old fears crowding back. She could imagine him approaching, and she looked round in sudden panic, noticing how empty the park was. She edged to her feet, then she was gone, gathering her books and walking off in one furtive movement. After that she avoided the park in the daytime, preferring to suffer the heat and discomfort of the college library. 'Anyway,' she told herself, 'it's easier to study in the library. At least you can't go to sleep with the librarian checking every few minutes.' Yet the man remained in her mind. She wondered who he was, what he had been doing there. It was unusual to see a black man dressed like that, let alone to come across one in the park at that time of day.

She was working full-time now, adding to her savings in the time between exams and university; waiting for her results in the sure knowledge that she could not fail. Yet when they came the sense of achievement swelled her heart. It was on the same morning her results came that she saw the man again. He had been standing by the clock tower, deep in conversation with another man. As Hyacinth passed on her way to work, he had looked up, recognised her and smiled. She had smiled back, feeling buoyed up by the good news, wanting to communicate her joy to someone, seeing in him a familiar face.

'He's not so bad,' she told herself as she turned down the small cobbled street leading away from the city centre.

He was there again the next morning, and for the rest of the week. He always smiled at her and they fell into a routine of nods and waves. Hyacinth got to look forward to seeing him; well-dressed and quiet, he seemed different from the rest, and soon she was weaving fantasies around him. Now, when she read her romantic novels, she would fancy that he was the hero, she the heroine; and it was always clean, and white and good. She dreamt of him approaching her, wining and dining her, taking her home . . . There the dream would falter, dissolving in the face of reality. The sordid hostel impinged on her consciousness, leaving her bitter and unhappy.

One morning she was woken by bright daylight shining in her eyes, and she sat up abruptly to the knowledge that she would be late for work. She had not expected to see him in the usual place, and she moved with brisk purpose across the road to the clock tower without bothering to look up.

'You're late.' The voice brought her to a skidding halt, her heart skipping with shock at the unexpected voice. He now stood in front of her, and irritation mingled with wariness as she pulled herself together. 'Don't you have to be at work by eight-thirty?' he asked now.

'I overslept,' she said automatically, a note of apology creeping into her voice.

'I could give you a lift in the mornings,' he suggested casually.

Hyacinth looked at him in surprise. 'I usually walk,' she said guardedly, not quite sure how to take this new turn of events. 'And anyway, I don't want to put you out.' She felt nervous and excited at the same time. In her mind she already knew him, but actually to have him talk to her, offer to give her a lift . . .

'I . . . I have to go to work now,' she said hastily, cutting off the direction of her thoughts.

'I'll walk with you,' he offered pleasantly.

'Don't you have to go to work?'

'I'm already late,' he said easily. 'I don't suppose a few more minutes will make much difference.'

She had been careful to keep the excitement out of her voice, but inside she felt warm at his persistence.

He was humorous, full of charm, and somehow she found herself agreeing to meet him after work the following evening. It was only to give her a lift home, but she looked forward to it, as if it was the date of her dreams.

He was waiting for her in a small blue mini, parked neatly outside the staff entrance of the supermarket where she worked. It was only when she saw the car that the implications of his taking her home occurred to her. She did not want him to find out where she lived, he would have nothing but contempt for her if he did. Yet she did not have the courage to tell him she had changed her mind and instead, slipped reluctantly into the seat beside him. She gave him the name of a street close to the hostel, but when he reached it, he did not stop.

'Where exactly do you live?' he asked. 'I don't mind dropping you.'

She was reluctant to tell him, but he had slowed to a stop in the middle of the road. Shame burned in her face as she told him, and she dared not look at him. She wondered if he would guess what her father had done, if he would ask her why she was at that hostel. She could tell from his silence that he had recognised the name. Everyone in Leicester had heard of the Lodge. There was hardly a day when the local papers did not carry a story about one or other of its residents. She was glad when the car finally stopped, relieved that he had not shamed her.

He was there the next morning when she came out of the hostel. Hyacinth felt the weight of rejection lifting. She had cried herself to sleep the night before, and her dreams had been filled with the nightmares from the past, all jumbled together with her father's face. Now, seeing him there, smiling cheerfully, the guilt slipped back, pushed far into the recesses of her mind. He made no mention of the hostel as he drove her to work, talked about himself instead. He told her his name was Mackay and that he worked as a structural engineer. Hyacinth was impressed. She wondered what a structural engineer was, figured it must be something important for him to own a car. Of course he picked her up from then on, and also took her home in the evenings. Hyacinth felt happy. Mackay was so nice. All he wanted to do was talk and he never made any attempt to be like her father.

It was on her last day at work that he invited her out. She told him as she joined him in the car, still a little shy in his company.

'I'm going down to Birmingham tomorrow,' she reminded him tentatively, feeling guilty about not doing so before. She had only mentioned it briefly once before, soon after they first met. He was silent for a long time, picking his way through the Saturday evening traffic.

102

'Let's go out and celebrate,' he said finally, in a carefully neutral voice.

She felt taken aback. He had never asked her out before, and she wondered if she ought to refuse.

'Well? Have you considered it enough?' he asked, after the silence had gone on for a while.

'I'd like that,' Hyacinth said, regretting it almost as soon as the words were out. A dull apprehension had started in her stomach, and she forced her mind away from thoughts of what she might be getting herself into. He is not like the rest, she told herself grimly, he's my friend, the only one I have in England.

Mackay took her to a small pub close to the hostel, and she was too polite to tell him that she disliked it. She had never been in a pub before and it made her feel tense and awkward. It was the sort of place she could imagine her father liking, and she found herself looking around apprehensively several times during the evening, peering through the smoke that made her eyes smart. She had dressed specially in a pink dress with shoe-string straps, her hair newly straightened to go to university. In the pub she felt overdressed and out of place, and she was sure people were looking at her. Yet she sat there, wedged into a corner, the smell of sweating bodies all around her as she tried to make out what he was saying over the noise of the rock music. She would have liked to ask to leave, and she breathed with relief when he finally made a move.

'I thought we could have dinner at my place,' he said casually, as he settled her comfortably into the car.

Hyacinth's heart skipped a beat, and a fluttering joined the queasiness left from the noisy, smoke-filled pub in her stomach. She sat still and silent as the car moved out of its parking space and turned away from the hostel. She wished she had the nerve to tell him to turn back, ask him to stop the car, anything but sit there in acceptance. She told herself how nice he was, how polite, but still the fear remained. If only she was the heroine in the book she was reading. She would know what to do then, she thought unhappily. Instead, she concentrated on how much she liked him, how much she trusted him.

Mackay lived in a flat in one of the better suburbs of the city, and Hyacinth was immediately at ease when she saw it. She felt safe there, loving the nice bright colours and the modern furniture. 'He's just like me,' she thought. 'Civilised and tasteful.' She thought she would never get tired of looking at the place, drinking in every detail avidly. There were fitted carpets everywhere, a nice, clean beige carpet that was like a fluffy cushion under her feet. It was like a dream, like the bedroom adverts on the television or the Dulux paint leaflets.

'Come and keep me company in the kitchen,' he suggested, as she stood in the middle of the lounge, not daring to sit on the new-looking cloth settee.

'It's a nice flat,' she ventured, as she eased herself gingerly onto one of the high stools in the fitted kitchen.

'Thanks.'

She did not know what else to say, and he did not seem to be in the mood for conversation as he concentrated on tossing the salad. She would have liked to offer her help but was too shy, and so she sat, playing with her fingers, feeling awkward in the silence.

'Why are you living in a rehabilitation hostel for young offenders?'

Hyacinth stiffened. He had not even straightened, or moved his attention from the salad. Shame and guilt seeped into her, and her scalp itched from embarrassment.

'I had nowhere to go when I left the children's home,' she said defensively.

'You were in a children's home?'

She had forgotten about not mentioning it, and the curiosity and surprise in his voice made her shrink into herself.

'Why were you in a children's home?' he asked after a pause.

Hyacinth shifted uncomfortably, wishing he would stop asking questions. She had been so sure he had accepted where she lived without question, and she wished she could have been spared this humiliation.

'My father and I didn't get on,' she mumbled defensively.

'You don't strike me as a difficult person,' he said, sounding surprised.

'I had a stepmother . . .' she started, but he cut her off.

'Say no more. That I can understand.'

She felt warm towards him, a sudden impulse to confide. The words burnt on her tongue, so intense she could almost taste the need to talk. But the thought of his contempt, the dislike she knew he would feel if he found out what her father had done, only that kept her silent.

They ate mackerel and green bananas, and Hyacinth hid her surprise when he set it on the table with the salad. She enjoyed it, lingering over the well-cooked fish, closing her eyes on the memory. The taste reminded her of Saturday evenings in Kingston, onions frying and a sun-bleached, grey wood shack . . . She pushed that from her mind, suddenly unsettled. How could a dream like that get mixed up with her memory? It made her uneasy, marred her enjoyment of the meal, and she was glad when they moved to the lounge with their coffee, glad to leave that too-familiar smell.

They talked in low voices, mainly about university. When he took her cup out of her hand, she looked up in surprise.

'I haven't finished,' she ventured helpfully.

He ignored her, putting the cup beside his on the coffee table.

'I find you very attractive, Hyacinth,' he said, in a voice that brought unpleasant echoes of Colin Matthews. She shifted uneasily beside him.

'I suppose it must be the dress,' she said, feeling awkward and uncomfortable, wishing with all her heart that she had not worn it.

When he kissed her fear ran along her veins, making it hard to breathe. She pulled herself away, and stumbling to her feet, eyed him with distrust and revulsion.

'Hey! What's the matter?' Mackay grabbed at her wrist, looking surprised.

'I have to go!' she responded, clawing frantically at his grasp with her free hand, feeling her palms wet with sweat.

'That may be,' he said, irritation coming into his voice. 'But first I want to know the game you're playing.'

Hyacinth felt the shaking start deep within her, and almost on reflex gritted her teeth to stop them chattering and pressed her knees together. 'God! Please don't let him hurt me!' she prayed desperately. 'Don't let him do what happened to Anne.'

He looked big and angry sitting there, his grip on her wrist so painful that her skin stretched and tautened in readiness for expected blows. She had a compulsion to look down, to see the lump she knew would be there, the anger she knew was waiting to burst out at her. His grip tightened.

'Anyone would think I was going to rape you,' he said bitterly. 'Why are you afraid of me? What have I done?'

She held herself stiffly, hardly daring to breathe, afraid the slightest movement would bring down his anger. He shook her slightly.

'What's the matter?' he asked impatiently.

'N . . . nothing. I have to go.'

He ignored that.

'If nothing is the matter then I might as well give you something,' he said, getting to his feet and pulling her to him. Fear churned about in her stomach like a physical thing: 'Incest flourished where the roads were bad!' The words reverberated in her head, causing the food to lurch about precariously in her stomach. She remembered it, big and obscene, rubbing against her belly. 'I'm going to be sick,' she thought in misery, body tensing further in the effort to force the salt out of her mouth.

The wet pressure of his mouth on hers made her gag, and she felt the tears smarting her eyes, running down her cheeks as his tongue invaded her mouth with wet determination. She struggled desperately, free hand clawing in panic at his face. Then she was free, stumbling backwards, watching him warily. He looked at her with contempt, and she stood, frozen with terror, unable to control the shaking in her limbs.

'I'll take you back,' he said finally, voice full of anger.

She would have liked to refuse, but she was afraid he might get upset, start again, and anyway she didn't even know where she was.

Never had the hostel looked so good.

'Thanks for a nice evening,' she said politely, when the car slid to a halt and she was safely on the pavement.

'I wish I could say the same,' he said flatly.

'I'm sorry.' She shifted awkwardly, feeling guilty and ashamed.

'Don't be,' he said with hostility. 'I can do without that; though if I were you, Hyacinth, I would stop being such a tease.'

Her eyes darted nervously across the empty street, and she bit back the denial that sprang to her lips. She was not quite sure what to do and she hovered on the pavement until he drove away.

Hyacinth came awake reluctantly to the insistent drumming of rain on the windowpane. She lay, suspended between sleeping and waking, half-listening to the sound. Her mind moved away, drifted from the thought of the leaden sky outside the thin green curtains. It was on a day like this that she had gone to the country with her aunt, and she smiled at the memory, eyes too heavy to open, too awake to be asleep, too asleep to be awake.

It was Easter and they were staying with Aunt Joyce's friend for the holidays. Hyacinth had never been to Buff Bay before. What she remembered most vividly was the sky, so heavy you could climb a coconut palm and touch it. That, and the water dancing and sliding off the new zinc roof. The sea, glimpsed through a crack in the wooden wall, looked savage, a wild and angry grey.

'You mus stay weh fram ihm,' Aunt Joyce told her solemnly, as they stood together on the veranda, hands firmly clasped, and looked out at the boiling depths, so different from Gunboat and Buccaneer beach. 'Is God son die today mek it stay soh. If you goh dung deh you naw come back.'

Hyacinth clutched the big, reassuring hand, heart fluttering, glad when her aunt retreated to the house. Back inside she had listened to the noise, straining on tiptoe to catch a glimpse of the water through the shuttered window as the rain came down in another hissing drive, pounding and dancing on the zinc roof. She could just see the waves foaming and boiling against the rocks through the shuttered window, and she shivered, coming down off her toes, glancing around.

'The wise man built his house upon the rocks, and the rain came tumbling down,' she sang under her breath.

She fancied the waves were throwing themselves harder at the rocks now, and she looked again in alarm. She could imagine them groping their way towards the cluster of wooden houses, waiting for her to turn away before rushing at them.

'Don't let them force us into the water,' she prayed desperately. 'I know your son died today, and I'm really sorry. Amen.'

She looked around swiftly, afraid her aunt would catch her, shout at her for being stupid; but she felt a little better for showing her sympathy.

Hyacinth sighed, turning over and snuggling further into the bed. It had been the only time her aunt had taken her to the countryside and she had been glad to return to Kingston. Fancy remembering that now, she thought, smiling at the little things which had frightened her then. Outside her room she could hear the house coming alive, the buzz of voices mingling with the rain and the muted roar of the traffic.

Eight

Hyacinth liked her room at college from the start. It was one of those curious–shaped rooms, all angles and jutting pieces of wall. The wallpaper had the drab, washed-out look she had come to associate with rented accommodation, while the carpet had long ago lost any trace of a pattern. Only the bookcase and the heater stood out, centred on the only unbroken piece of wall. She loved the room though. Loved its uneven symmetry, even the orange curtains, jangling and discordantly loud. It was the kind of room she imagined a student should live in. A shabby, bookish room, practical yet full of interest. Outside, she could hear the discreet sound of cultured voices, so different from the swearing and the coarseness she had grown used to. Not even the rain, which had fallen almost constantly since she arrived, could dampen her spirit. She was warm and comfortable in her room, with its fitted carpet. She even had a friend. As usual the last thought made her swell with pride. She, Hyacinth, had a Jamaican friend. She sometimes wondered what Perlene saw in her, why she bothered to waste so much of her time with her.

They had met in the students' union building. Hyacinth had been sitting in a corner of the common-room, reading a book, when a heavily accented Jamaican voice had interrupted her flow.

'Which part of Jamaica you come from?'

'Kingston,' she had said automatically, looking up in surprise. 'How did you know I was from Jamaica?'

The girl had curled her long body into the seat beside her, a grin on her face. 'There is only a few of us here, and someone mentioned that you were Jamaican as well.'

Hyacinth nodded, thinking enviously that there was no mistaking where the other girl came from. Hyacinth had given herself a new identity since coming to Aston, mindful of the shameful secrets in her past, and had deliberately created an image she thought other people would envy. It made her confident to come from a good background, to know that none of them could look at her with pity, or guess the secret she carried in her heart. She found that she could talk to the other students now, could get on with them on equal terms. At the same time she avoided the male students, wary after her last mistake. At times she still felt cautious and timid, still feared ridicule. But Perlene would not allow this, refused to let Hyacinth stay in her shell. Hyacinth deeply envied the other girl's confidence, the way she was so unguarded and full of life, tumbling unheedingly into every new experience.

'I really miss home,' Perlene had confided the first time they met, and Hyacinth had warmed to her.

'I know what you mean,' she had volunteered shyly, liking the other's friendly directness. They were both in the first year, and Hyacinth was surprised to find that the other girl was a year younger than her. 'Did you come straight from Jamaica?' she asked, in a carefully neutral voice.

'More or less,' Perlene replied easily. 'I've been staying with some of my mother's people in London since last month.'

'What do you think of it?' Hyacinth asked curiously, hoping the girl didn't mind being questioned, hungry for anything she could learn. Perlene moved her thin shoulders expressively, wrinkling her nose at the same time.

'England too cold and wet for my use,' she said slowly. 'And the people them don't like black people too much; but aside from that it's all right.' She grinned at her own humour, before turning the question back. 'What about you, Hyacinth, how long have you been in England?'

'Oh, only a few years,' Hyacinth said hastily, guilt and tension displacing her feeling of ease and well-being. She laughed self-consciously. 'I pick up accents really quickly,' she added on a defensive note. She had never tried out her new identity on a Jamaican before and she was afraid Perlene would guess her secret. The other girl looked at her oddly, and she rushed on, aware that she was talking too much, yet none the less needing to convince her. 'I know I sound really native,' she said now, 'but it always happen. When I was in the States it was the same thing and even my aunt, who I live with, used to laugh at me.' She felt her nerves stretching as the other girl frowned and seemed about to say something; her relief was almost audible when she seemed to change her mind and smiled instead.

They had become firm friends, Hyacinth relaxing as much as she could with the lie she had created after the initial difficulty had passed. Thankfully, Perlene loved to talk, and the occasional 'yes' from her was generally all that was expected. Perlene came from Annatto Bay and Hyacinth loved hearing her talk about the town, and St Mary in general. 'It's not a bad place,' Perlene said once, 'at least compared to Kingston.' 'It's not a city at all,' Hyacinth corrected, emboldened by her success with the other girl so far, stung by the criticism of her beloved city, 'and Kingston is a really nice place,' she continued. 'If you lived in England for a while you would soon stop knocking it.'

'Girl, you must wear blinkers,' Perlene snorted rudely. 'You mean you don't even read the headlines in the papers? Them political madmen a mash up Kingston with the gun-war.'

'I don't listen to what the papers say,' Hyacinth answered, shifting uncomfortably, sure she could detect slight contempt in the piercing, lively eyes. She knew that Perlene had the Jamaican daily papers sent to her, had sometimes glanced at them, but she found it hard to believe what they were saying. She could understand why the British newspapers carried such awful stories about Jamaica — white people never did like Jamaicans, and it was little wonder they did all they could to attack Jamaica.

'I suppose you follow Manley's "Lead and I Follow" method of politics,' Perlene had said scathingly, during another argument. Hyacinth did not know much about Manley. It was only since meeting Perlene that she had found out he was Jamaica's prime minister, and it had taken her even longer to realise that he was not the Norman Manley that her aunt had often talked about, but his son. Not that she let on about her ignorance, preferring to nod in agreement, or keep quiet during discussion, while drinking in as much knowledge as she could. What she did find out about

Manley, she liked. He had been elected to govern Jamaica, and the Americans and a white man born in America, named Seaga, wanted him out. She had seen a picture of Manley in the *Guardian* and thought he looked really nice. He had beautiful skin and the sort of 'pass for white' colour she had always wanted. She felt resentful that the American CIA should try to kill him, and hated the way her friend mocked his marriage to a dark-skinned woman.

'Listen,' she told Perlene in exasperation, 'I don't believe Manley is doing anything bad to Jamaica. As far as I can see, the CIA and people like you are just giving him a bad name to get rid of him.'

Perlene looked superior. 'I am not denying that Manley bit off more than he could chew,' she conceded, 'but that's no excuse for the way he is selling my people to protect his class interest.'

Hyacinth did not understand that, she only knew that the anger was bubbling up inside her at the attack. 'I don't know how you can go around letting people think you're so black and still support a white man,' she snapped. 'Everybody knows that Seaga don't like black people.'

Perlene hissed impatiently through her teeth, 'Get your head out of your test-tube and take a look at the real world for once, Hyacinth.'

'You don't have to study politics to understand it,' Hyacinth threw back. 'Just because you are a Seaga supporter, don't mean Manley is wrong.'

Perlene looked furious, the amicable discussion rapidly getting out of hand. 'Don't be so simplistic,' she snapped back. 'Just because I don't support Manley don't mean that I support Seaga. This is one of the same attitudes that is mashing up the country. I mean, even though Manley is Jamaican he has no more interest in African people than Seaga does. They all belong to the same side.'

'Why should he care about Africans anyway?' Hyacinth asked, diverted. She could not understand what Perlene was talking about now. As far as she could see, Jamaica had enough problems without taking on other people's as well. Black people were always looking for something to criticise in other people. Perlene was looking at her in disbelief.

'You better realise that it's Africans like you and me who represent Jamaica's future,' she said forcefully. 'I tell you,

Hyacinth, when my father talk about how dread things were in his day, I just glad Buckra day nearly done.'

Hyacinth looked at her friend in amazement. Everybody knew Buckra's day had ended in 1962, when Jamaica got its independence from England. Even Perlene must remember that. She supposed it was because the other girl came from the country that she didn't know much history; but she was too tactful to correct her. 'Anyway, I am not an African,' she said, going back to the earlier point. Perlene laughed mirthlessly. 'Of course you are an African,' she said impatiently. 'If you aren't, what are you?'

'I am a Jamaican, of course; or a West Indian if you prefer.'

'Does that mean Nigerians and Ghanaans are not Africans, since they are Nigerians or Ghanaans?'

'That's different, and you know it.'

Perlene raised her eyes heavenward in an exaggerated gesture of impatience. 'How is that different? Can't you see how they brainwash you? Africans are the only race of people who are ashamed of their origin. Caucasians are Caucasians, Chinese are Chinese, but Africans, Africans are negroes, or West Indians or anything else that don't mean African. What's the matter with you, Hyacinth, why don't you admit what you are and be proud of it?'

Hyacinth hated conversations like these, where she was left feeling exposed and small. Yet she courted them, learning more and more about black people, in a way liking her friend's pride and courage. There was so much she did not not know, and one of her fears was that one day the other girl would find out. Already Perlene looked at her strangely sometimes, almost as if she had something she wanted to challenge her about. Many times she would brace herself, stomach clenched in expectation as she waited for the axe of discovery to fall.

'It will be better when I get to Jamaica,' she often told herself. 'When I am back with Aunt Joyce, none of them can say anything to me.'

Quite a few other people shared Perlene's views on Jamaica, and despite her protests that she did not want to listen to the constant criticism, the other girl insisted on dragging her to the meetings held by the black students on the campus. It was all so new, so alien. She had thought that she was unique among black people,

112

that her education set her apart. Yet these people seemed more interested in going back to the primitiveness they had come from. Everyone seemed to be in the business of reclaiming their history, and she found the idea of Africans having civilisations too far-fetched to believe. But every time she raised objections, Perlene would find another book for her to read, more pictures to convince her, and slowly, reluctantly, she was forced to rethink. They were strange, these black people, but grudgingly she learnt to respect them and, to her surprise, even seek them out. She still could not bring herself to consider people from Africa her equals, but was prepared to compromise by accepting that her people came originally from that continent.

Winter came to the campus, bringing biting winds and a bleak emptiness to the landscape. Hyacinth huddled in her duffle coat, gritting her teeth against the icy winds as she hurried from her hall to the teaching block. All around her, the other students were beginning to pair up, jumping into the mating game with the same vigour and energy as they had dived into radical politics. She felt an outsider, shut out by her lack of understanding and her fears. Always she would listen to the politics from the sidelines, always she would dodge the sexual games, fear in the form of her father lurking in the corner of her mind, waiting for his chance to spring. Even Perlene had found a man, and Hyacinth felt a sense of betrayal as she saw them, huddled close together, walking slowly along in their private world. She was disappointed in her friend, but had told herself that it was only because of the man she had chosen. He was a big, athletic Kenyan with a public-school accent and she wished he had at least been West Indian. They had invited her out once or twice and at first she had accepted, not wanting to hurt her friend's feelings. On these occasions she sat silent, resisting all of Perlene's attempts to draw her into the conversation. She knew the Kenyan disliked her, and she returned the feeling in full measure. She hated his accent, the way he always seemed to dress like an exaggerated English gentleman. He was such a contradiction, sipping gin and tonic and talking about the African revolution.

By the time summer came, Perlene and her Kenyan were an established part of life. Hyacinth had resigned herself to seeing less of her friend, and had even managed to make casual friends with some of the students in her chemistry classes. She was sitting at her desk one day, idly leafing through a book, eyes unfocused as her mind drifted away from the complicated problem in front of her. The door crashed inwards, banging against the wall with a shudder, causing Hyacinth to jump as the shock ran through her. Perlene came in, eyes bright with excitement.

'Hyacinth, you'll never guess what!'

'What?' Hyacinth asked with faint irritation, heart still beating unsteadily. She had not seen the other girl for almost a week, and now she had nearly frightened the life out of her.

'Dr Walter Rodney is coming to give a lecture!'

The thin face was animated, the eyes full of excitement and anticipation.

'That's nice,' Hyacinth said, feeling totally at a loss. Who on earth was Walter Rodney? She had certainly never heard of him. She supposed he had something to do with Perlene's course. Yet other people had come to give lectures before and she had never seen the other girl in such a state.

Perlene looked at her in horror. 'What do you mean "that's nice"?' she asked in amazement. '*The* Walter Rodney is coming here, and all you can say is "that's nice". Girl, don't you know who Walter Rodney is?'

The incredulity in Perlene's voice made Hyacinth squirm, but she could see no point in denying her ignorance. Perlene shook her head, hands aggressively on her hips.

'Walter Rodney is one of the best African historians around, girl. He did cause some trouble in Jamaica back in '68. He might not be another Garvey, but he sure is as good in his own way.'

Hyacinth knew she was looking blank. She felt hopelessly ignorant, but none of what Perlene said made much sense to her. The way Perlene talked about this Walter Rodney guy, she obviously expected her to have heard of him, but she had never even heard the name.

'Don't you remember when Shearer's government tried to ban Rodney?' Perlene persisted. Shearer? She had never heard of him either. She could vaguely remember Donald Sangster being prime minister after Busta, and dying of something or other, but this name was a new one to her. Perlene sighed dramatically. 'This girl

114

suppose to be born and grow a yard and she don't even know what happen around her.' Hyacinth felt her stomach lurch, nervous sweat breaking out in her palms. Did Perlene know? Was that what she was trying to say? She was always so quick on the uptake. Maybe she knew and was just keeping quiet about it for the time being. 'All right, let me tell you a bit about Walter Rodney,' Perlene said with resigned tolerance. Hyacinth flinched, feeling inadequate, but did not dare to protest as the other girl launched into speech. 'Walter Rodney is one dread academic when it come to African history. He is giving back African history to African people, radicalising the way it is written and creating a tool, a potential force for liberation.' Hyacinth nodded, not really understanding, but realising that Perlene would not appreciate the interruption. 'The man write some hard things,' Perlene continued, 'challenge a lot of the white racism written into African history. He's been teaching in Africa for years; and if it's the last thing you do, you going to read one of his books.' Hyacinth was not so sure about that. She found a lot of the books Perlene insisted she read hard to understand. She didn't even know how white racism had got into African history, indeed this was the first she had heard of it and she was sure reading this Walter Rodney book would not make her any the wiser. At the same time, she did not like the sound of the man. Fancy causing trouble in Jamaica! She would not be surprised if he had been working for the Americans.

'What will he be talking about?' she asked, forcing enthusiasm into her voice, trying to distract the other girl.

'Racism in Britain and its echoes in the Caribbean.'

Hyacinth bristled. There was no racism in the Caribbean, and anyway a man who taught in Africa was hardly qualified to talk on the British situation. She was getting fed up of these endless lectures, feeling saturated with all this business of black achievements. As far as she could see, that was in the past and it was certainly not helping much with the present. She was careful not to show any sign of what she was thinking, knowing from experience what her friend's reaction would be.

'Why don't you go with John?' she asked hopefully, trying to distract Perlene with a mention of the Kenyan. 'He seems to know so much about these things. I'm sure you will enjoy it better with him.'

Perlene shrugged her shoulders, anger flashing briefly in her eyes. 'Don't even mention him to me,' she said crossly. 'Do you know what the dog said to me?' Hyacinth shook her head, hiding her amusement at the sudden change of mood. 'He had the nerve to tell me that women were only good for one thing, and if he couldn't get it with me he had to go elsewhere.'

'The nerve,' Hyacinth said sympathetically. 'I hope you told him off.'

'Oh, I told him to go get it from someone else,' Perlene said heatedly, and Hyacinth nodded with satisfaction as the other added in disgust, 'And do you know, he went.'

'So what are you going to do now?' Hyacinth asked curiously.

'Do!' Perlene sounded incredulous. 'Why nothing, of course. To tell the truth I was getting a bit fed up of the whole English gentleman routine,' she confided, looking far from broken-hearted. 'Not even the English act like that; at least not the ones I've met, at any rate.' She looked at Hyacinth closely, changing the subject with her usual disregard. 'So you're coming then.' It was less a question than a statement, and Hyacinth nodded helplessly, feeling that she had no choice.

The lecture was good. To Hyacinth's surprise Dr Rodney seemed to know exactly what was going on in England. She found herself sitting forward as he talked about discrimination in schools and housing, remembering the squalor of her father's house with fresh understanding. It brought back other memories too. The teachers turning a blind eye to her misery, the abuse and assaults at the children's home and, even more painful, her stay in the hostel for young offenders. They were raw wounds that he exposed, the fear and frustration of having nowhere to turn to as fresh as if it had been yesterday. She found his analysis a bit of an anticlimax, though. It was all well and good blaming capitalism for the housing, but what had that to do with why the white kids had picked on her so mercilessly at school and at the children's home, or why white people hated black people so much?

When he spoke about the Caribbean it was another matter entirely. How could he make a comparison between the furtive, unacknowledged racism of British society and any legacy of hate in the Caribbean? Hyacinth's annoyance was deepened by Perlene's obvious agreement. How could her friend sit there and agree while her own country was being condemned? 'I bet that stupid Kenyan did this to her,' she thought in irritation. She herself could remember Jamaica perfectly and the one thing she had to say about it was that racism did not exist there. She supposed there might be some prejudice among the more ignorant people, but it was certainly nothing compared to Britain, and Jamaicans never meant any harm anyway. 'It's such a biased attack,' she thought angrily, flinching at the number of times he used the Jamaican situation to illustrate his point. As far as she could see, he was probably being vindictive because they had caught him making trouble in the sixties.

At the end of the talk she was so angry, she would have walked off without speaking to Perlene, but the other girl chased after her, brushing aside her coldness with characteristic disregard. 'Hey, hold on a minute,' she said, hanging on to Hyacinth's reluctant arm. 'I was going to see if I could meet Walter Rodney.'

'You do that,' Hyacinth said stiffly, unable to keep her dissatisfaction out of the words. 'I have other things to do.'

'What's wrong with you now?' Perlene asked impatiently. 'Don't tell me you didn't agree with what Rodney was saying?'

'What right did he have to single out Jamaica?' she answered, anger bubbling over. 'He's like a traitor to black people.'

'Don't be so dramatic,' Perlene said, her voice suddenly thoughtful. 'He was perfectly right about the Jamaican situation, you know.'

Hyacinth disliked the gentle certainty in her friend's voice, pushed back the panicky feeling that what she was saying might be the truth.

'You're biased, you like him anyway,' she said desperately.

Perlene shook her head. 'I grew up in Jamaica, Hyacinth,' she said gently. 'Racism is deep in the place. Have you ever wondered how it is that with a predominantly black population we should be governed by so many 'pass for white' and white men?'

The question took her off-guard, went right to the centre of her hidden dissatisfaction, and she shifted uncomfortably, refusing to allow it to penetrate. 'You don't know what you are talking about,' she denied. 'Jamaica is a democracy. Everybody has free choice.'

Perlene laughed bitterly. 'I hardly call a gun in your back free

117

choice. And if the political banditry going on in Jamaica is what you call democracy, I'm not surprised so much of the Third World don't believe in it.'

Hyacinth felt her jaw aching from anger and shock.

'No wonder you're always knocking Jamaica,' she said, her voice reflecting her surprise. 'Honestly, Perlene, you are like a Russian propaganda machine.'

'Don't you mean American?' came the calm response. 'After all, we are supposed to be socialist — or have you forgotten? But just because Manley has decided he is a socialist, don't mean I am going to fall into line like some left-wing group and give him uncritical support.'

'Ladies! Ladies! It is a shame to see such good friends arguing.'

Hyacinth swung round to see a slender man, not much taller than herself, standing behind them. Perlene's face lit up, argument forgotten.

'Charles!' she exclaimed, flinging herself at the man and hugging him. 'Where have you been? You just missed one dread lecture.'

Charles smiled in acknowledgement. 'Then you will no doubt tell me all about it another time,' he said gravely before adding, 'Will you not introduce me to your friend?'

'Oh, this is Hyacinth,' Perlene said, turning to include the other girl. Hyacinth had heard Perlene talk about Charles. He was a postgraduate student from Rhodesia, which she insisted on calling Zimbabwe. He had been forced to leave his own country because of his political activities, and was studying for the day when his country won its freedom. He had a cold, neglected look about him, and she felt a fellowship, a sympathy for him, as he smiled at her. She knew what it was like to be an exile. When she had first come to Aston, she had felt contempt for the Southern Africans, amazed that so few whites could keep so many black people in bondage. Now, meeting them, talking to them, she wondered if she would have the courage to risk death as many of them seemed prepared to do. Until then she had not really taken their fight seriously, but after that she had felt a sense of guilt at the South African oranges and grapes sitting in her fruit bowl. She had salved her conscience by dumping them in the bin, feeling righteous about the waste. Yet still her feeling of superiority had persisted. As far as she was

concerned the situation could not have happened in Jamaica —
look how they had forced the British to end slavery.

Autumn brought with it a new intake of students and a flurry of
black activities. There was an African week, which was basically a
series of political lectures and cultural events, as well as a variety of
exhibitions. Hyacinth was beginning to feel irritated by the
constant preoccupation with politics. It was like an unyielding and
uncompromising religion whose dogma she could not understand.
She felt sensitive about Jamaica. It seemed to be on everyone's lips
and none of the Jamaicans had a single good thing to say. They
were either pro-Seaga or plain anti-Manley. She would have liked
to defend the prime minister, and sometimes, heart pounding,
body shaking with tension, she would gear herself up to speak,
only to find the words slipping away when it came to the test. She
listened to talk after talk on Manley's Jamaica, rasta and reggae,
and finally it all came to a head.

'What's the matter with everyone?' she asked Perlene angrily.
'Why do you all knock everything good about Jamaica and push
everything bad?'

'What's bothering you now?' Perlene sighed. 'I thought you said
you were enjoying the week.'

'I would if they would stop pushing socialism and knocking my
country; I hate rastas, think reggae is boring, and support Manley,
OK?'

They were in Hyacinth's room, Perlene sitting on the bed, with
her feet curled under her. 'Why don't you accept the truth about
Jamaica, Hyacinth?' she sighed, leaning back against the wall.
'Your ignorance is plain to see.'

'What do you mean?' Hyacinth asked defensively, heart leaping
with anxiety.

Perlene looked angry with herself. 'It doesn't matter,' she said
shortly, adding hastily, 'Look, I'd better go and leave you with
your work.'

Hyacinth felt the panic rising inside her as the girl groped
around under the bed for her shoes. Supposing she knew? She just
had to know, had to find out what Perlene was driving at. 'Wait!'
she said, as the girl made for the door. Perlene looked back.
'You're a bit upset,' she said placatingly. 'Let's talk about it
another time.' She was through the door before Hyacinth could

119

say anything else. Feeling desperate, Hyacinth kicked off her slippers, struggling into her shoes with fearful haste. She just had to know, had to find out. Perlene was half-way down the sloping path by the time Hyacinth caught her. 'What do you mean by my ignorance?' she asked breathlessly, grabbing one of the girl's swinging hands. Perlene halted in mid-stride, giving Hyacinth a curious look.

'It doesn't matter,' she said easily. 'It was just a figure of speech.'

'It matters to me,' Hyacinth persisted stubbornly. 'You can't just say something like that and walk away.'

'For God sake,' Perlene burst out. 'Christ, Hyacinth, stop being so intense.'

'Well tell me then,' Hyacinth replied grimly.

The other girl threw up her hands in defeat and in that instant Hyacinth saw Charles approaching them.

'It doesn't matter,' she said hastily, sensing disaster, knowing what the other girl was about to reveal.

Perlene had not seen the approaching Charles. 'You might as well know, seeing as it means so much,' she said with irony. 'The truth is, Hyacinth, that everybody knows you are ignorant about Jamaica. It's obvious that you haven't been there for years. You don't even know basic things about the country which have nothing to do with which party you support.'

Hyacinth stared at her in shock, the knowledge that Charles had probably heard making her want to die.

'It's nice to know what you have been saying behind my back,' she said bitterly, the revelation making her feel ten times worse than she had expected.

'Don't be so stupid . . .' Perlene started, trailing off when she saw Charles. 'Look, no one was talking about you,' she finished lamely, looking at a loss for once.

Hyacinth stared mulishly, ignoring the plea in the other's voice. 'I know what I know,' she blustered. 'And if anyone don't like it that's their affair.' She felt sick with her own stupidity. She should have guessed that they would all be the same. Even Perlene had proved to be no different from the rest.

'Hyacinth, listen,' Perlene pleaded. But she ignored her, turning and walking away. 'I should have told you, but I didn't want to hurt your feelings,' the other said, stopping her in her tracks. 'Look, you insisted on knowing,' she continued rapidly. 'You keep talking about going back to Jamaica, but it was never a paradise, Hyacinth. Now it's wicked. Jamaica mash up, Hyacinth. If you going back, for God sake, know what you going back to.'

'Perlene, there is no need for that.' Charles' voice cut across the other girl's flow, causing Hyacinth to spin round in surprise, forgetting the tears that had traced rivulets down her face. 'You and Hyacinth have different interpretations, that is all,' he said firmly. 'I too romanticise aspects of my country when I feel homesick. There is no harm in it, so long as I know the reality.'

Perlene said nothing, looking relieved by the intervention; and this time when Hyacinth turned to go, she made no attempt to stop her. She felt grateful to Charles, though she brushed aside the doubts his words conjured. She knew the reality of Jamaica. Didn't her aunt always say it would never change? Jamaica was not Zimbabwe. Her country was not at war.

Nine

They sat on the hard dirt floor of the wooden shack, talking in low whispers, the busy sounds of evening seeping through the board walls. The kerosene lamp had long gone out, but the smell lingered unpleasantly on the cooling air. Hyacinth felt the unyielding grittiness press into her bottom. It made her ache, distracted her from what the other girls were saying. She thought longingly of the soft white settee in the large front room at home. It was too late to go back now, the street would be full of shadows and lurking men. They were talking in low voices, and Hyacinth moved closer to Florence as they started swopping duppy stories. She could feel the darkness pressing in on her, full of shadows and waiting fears, and she wondered how she would sleep in the narrow bed that night. After every story there was a pause, and they would all listen, eyes straining, trying to see through the cracks in the splintering knotty wood. Hyacinth listened intently, heart racing, body tensing every time she heard a footfall. She wished there was not such a long gap between the stories, wished she had never come. She knew he was out there lurking, waiting to spring on her, to expose her to the world. 'I have to go to the toilet,' she thought in panic. 'I have to go.' Desperation clawed at her as the thought hit her. How could she go out there alone? She thought of the shed at the far end of the yard, the darkness that separated her. If only she had not come, had kept to where she belonged.

She had always hated Lumber Street, and yet she always came. The sound of the bolts pulling back, squeaking in rusty protest as they finally gave way, brought her back to present danger.

'There's no harm in it, so long as you know the reality,' Cynthia said, looking at Hyacinth with pity; and then she was exposing her nakedness, moving away, abandoning her. She had to struggle to stop the urine coming down as he loomed above her, the lump menacing and exposed. She scrambled backwards on her bottom, knowing it was too late, that he had tainted her already. Then she was on her feet, was running to get away. But it was too late, he had divided into three, surrounded her.

Hyacinth came awake abruptly, sitting up in panic, feeling the shock of the dream reverberate inside her. She snapped the desk-light on with a shaky hand, the other feeling blindly under the covers, tension and horror in the blind, seeking motion. The bed was dry! Relief brought relaxation and the knowledge that her bladder was full to bursting point. She scrambled out of bed, dashed for the toilet next door. There she sat, head in hands, unable to dispel the nightmare street, the dream bringing vivid memory, digging it up from the recesses of her mind.

Fancy remembering Lumber Street now, she thought to herself. Had she really hated it, or was it since the fire? She could remember it now, see the flickering orange tongues of flame against the evening sky. Had she watched it alone, or did her friends see it too? She could not remember, could only remember the fire. It had happened so many years ago. Far, half-forgotten in the deep recesses of childhood, and yet in her memory it could have been yesterday. She saw it all behind her tightly closed lips, the hard-faced man, the little girl's scream of terror, the way it choked, gurgled off. Had it been her, she wondered?

It had been a funny kind of summer when it happened — dry and snappy. The heat had burned anger into the still air that clung to you as you forced your legs to move. She had walked past that house so many times, always wanting to see what mysteries lurked behind the wooden fence. It had been a disappointing summer, spent stealing mangoes and seeking coolness in the crumbling redness of the dry, forbidden gully. The thought of evening had always worried her, filled her with guilt that she could not take her friends home.

Yet the street had been a magnet, full of life and things best left unseen. It was the only place she was allowed where you could see dominoes played as it should be. Fat men, sweat seeping through their clothes, dripping down shiny noses, trapped in the creases of their bodies, as they hunched with concentration over the small black bricks. If she concentrated she could still see them, shirts open to reveal torn and aged singlet vests, one man occasionally rising, breaking the near silence with a yell and a slam. She could see them round the peeling grey wooden table, its legs gnawed and splintered by the fat, obscene rats that fed off the tenement waste. She could remember it all, the stain on the corner where the man had stabbed his wife to death, a spot to be avoided because of the vengeful ghost. And then there was the coolie-man shop, the familiar sounds of jukebox music coming from the dark mysterious doorways.

Yes, that summer had been truly hot, draining the blueness from the sky, leaching the moisture from the ground till it cracked and crumbled underfoot. It was the first time she had seen heat dance and shimmer like a living thing. It had burned her soles, plastered the thin frock to her back. Then there had been the ragged boys, laughing and jeering as she hopped in the heat, their bare feet slapping against the ground with hardened unconcern.

A knock on the door made her jump, jerked her out of her contemplation. She was not really sorry to let the street slip back. She had never really been at home there, and it was full of unhappy memories. But that was not Jamaica, she told herself stoutly, that was only one street, and it proved she knew the unpleasant side of Jamaica as well. The thought pleased her, renewed her faith. Of course she knew Jamaica. After all, she had grown up there too. She felt her tiredness recede a little, that deep-in-the-bone tired feeling giving place to a little hope, a little bit of belonging. Not that she could forgive Perlene her betrayal, but at least inside herself she knew the other's accusations were unfounded.

Hyacinth woke to an insistent knocking on her door and sunlight against her eyelids. She lay disoriented for a moment, not sure of where she was, the dream images slow to leave her head. Before she could move, the door opened and Charles put his head round.

'Perlene asked me to come and see if you were OK,' he said, hovering in the doorway, looking uncertain of his welcome.

'That's nice of her,' Hyacinth said coldly, the previous day's bitterness rearing up inside her. 'Well, now you've seen you can go and put her mind at rest.'

He came further into the room, his face concerned. 'That is not nice, Hyacinth,' he said reprovingly. 'She cares for you, as you well know. She did not intend that you should be hurt yesterday.'

Hyacinth's mouth compressed with anger. Fancy sending Charles to talk to her! He might be all right, and she might like him, but he was an African and this was a private thing between Perlene and herself.

'May I sit down?' he asked, ignoring her rudeness, and she shrugged noncommittally. Charles took that for assent, and once seated on her chair, changed the subject entirely. Hyacinth was surprised by his sudden change of tone, but she listened, interested despite herself. 'When I came to England I was so unhappy,' he said softly, looking at her with a gentle smile. 'I remember it was winter and I only had the thin coat I had left Botswana in. We had fled there, my family and I. But the unhappiness I had then was nothing compared with the feeling of being in a hostile and cold country.' He paused, looking at her hesitantly, as if he was picking his words with care. 'I remember . . . at nights . . . the eagerness with which I would seek my bed. You see, sometimes I would dream of being still in Zimbabwe in the days before joining the freedom-fighters. It was always so nice, so safe and happy in my dreams, and sometimes when I woke, I would think for a moment that it was real. It was easy in my loneliness to get dreams and reality mixed up, you see.'

Hyacinth looked at him with new understanding, new respect. It was so much like her own experience. Though it was always the nightmare of poverty that dogged her waking hours and she certainly could never mistake that for reality. She could feel herself relaxing, some of the shame-induced tensions seeping out of her. Charles was nice, he really understood the sort of person she was.

'Will you talk to Perlene?' he asked hopefully.

Hyacinth sighed. 'I suppose I will, eventually,' she said flatly.

'And won't spend this evening with her? Don't spend your Friday evenings together?'

'Not tonight,' she said with finality. 'I don't want to face her at the moment.'

'Will you come to the coffee shop with me then?' he asked hopefully.

A vision of Mackay flashed through her mind, hastily suppressed. Charles was different, he was certainly not aggressive and disgusting like Jamaican men. He had never made a pass at her, and she had been alone with him before, though she had never been out with him.

The evening had been a success, with Charles coming back to her room for coffee afterwards. They had talked until the early hours and she had been surprised at his ability to sustain conversation. She felt at ease in his company, and was quite happy to agree to another date. No, she didn't mind Charles. Small and thin, he was the exact opposite of her father. She felt safe with him, secure in the knowledge that she was West Indian, he a mere African. It made her feel good, important, and she took to spending a lot of time in his company.

She had tried talking to Perlene, but the other girl had not even attempted to see her side of things. 'I'll never forgive you or trust you again,' she had said, with frosty dignity, 'but we can continue where we left off.' 'Continue . . . where . . . we . . . left off!' Perlene had spluttered, the words strung out in surprise and anger. 'What you going on about now, Hyacinth? What exactly am I supposed to have done?' Hyacinth had been too furious to answer, had simply turned and walked away. How dare she pretend she didn't know what it was about, that she could so soon forget what she had done, the way she had talked the day before? She didn't need Perlene, she had Charles now. He might be a little quieter and a little too serious, but at least he never made fun of her behind her back.

She loved to hear him talk about the struggle for freedom in Zimbabwe.

'One thing I feel glad about is that we don't get that in Jamaica,' she told him once. 'At home people really like their freedom.'

Charles gave her an odd smile. 'But your country must still struggle against domination, surely?' he asked gently. 'You are still facing the problems of imperialism and neo-colonialism.'

Hyacinth shook her head, confident in his presence.

'It's not like Africa you know,' she said confidingly. 'People are more civi . . . well, aware of what freedom and independence mean.'

'You were going to say civilised, and yet we are the same people, Hyacinth.' he said sadly. 'European civilisation is a poor yardstick for development.'

Hyacinth shifted in embarrassment. She had not wanted to hurt his feelings by telling him the truth, as she saw it. 'I am not trying to say Africans are not civilised,' she said hastily. 'Only that we don't have any tribalism in the Caribbean.'

He shook his head wryly. 'Watch that when you go back to your island, you are not disappointed, Hyacinth,' he said gravely.

It was the day before her twenty-second birthday that she had gone to his flat. 'It's my birthday tomorrow,' she had told him on impulse. He was the closest friend she had, they had known each other for two years, and she suddenly felt the need to share her birthday with him.

'Why did you not tell me?' he asked chidingly, and she knew he did not just mean that year.

'I'm telling you now,' she said lightly.

'But I shall not be able to get you a present,' he said, adding on a sudden note, 'I know, you shall return tomorrow and I shall make dinner for you.'

Charles was a good cook and they ate well, though she was secretly relieved that instead of the outlandish Zimbabwean meal she had been expecting, he presented her with a very English stew.

126

Afterwards he made real coffee. 'A very special treat for poor students,' he smiled, handing her a mug and coming to sit beside her on the worn settee, stretching his legs out on the soiled mustard-yellow carpet. Hyacinth smiled lazily back. Her stomach felt full of warm contentment, her mind sluggish with satisfaction.

'Have you ever had a boyfriend?' Charles' question was low, matter-of-fact, bringing her back from her half-awake state.

'No,' she said, pulling a face. 'And I don't intend to get one either.' Visions of Mackay filtered into her mind, and she pushed them out ruthlessly.

'What happened, Hyacinth?'

She stiffened, for one awful moment thinking he had read her thoughts. 'What do you mean?' she asked evasively, eyes sliding away.

'I mean, what happened to turn you so away from men?' he persisted. 'And do not tell me it is not true. You are the only girl on the campus that seems to be about to take flight when a man approaches.'

'Nothing happened,' she said guardedly. 'And if I am so afraid of men, how comes we've been friends for so long?'

'Because you think of me as safe.' He hesitated, then seemed to come to a decision. 'We have been friends for two years, Hyacinth, and yet yesterday was the first time you came to my flat, and that only after I had invited you times without end. Is that what happened? Did a man invite you to his flat and attack you?'

Hyacinth nodded in relief, visions of her father beating at her mind. She was frightened that he might guess the truth. Charles saw too much, and she clutched greedily at the straw he had thrown her. She told him about Mackay, recounted the story with remembered anger.

'I think you overreacted,' Charles said without much sympathy, and she felt disappointed in him. 'He don't understand,' she thought in irritation. 'He is just a man after all.' 'What I want to know is, what happened to cause you to act in that manner to this man?'

The fear of discovery crept into her belly and she felt suddenly angry with him. 'What do you want me to say?' she snapped. 'I've told you what happened already.'

'You mean you had no idea this man found you attractive?' he persisted.

'I never gave him any encouragement,' she said stubbornly.

'You went out with him, went back to his flat.'

Hyacinth laughed mirthlessly. 'In that case, Charles, I must really be leading you on. I've been out with you a lot of times and I'm in your flat now.'

'That is a different thing,' he said mildly. 'But what makes you so sure I am not attracted to you?'

'You're joking!' she said, anger mixing with sudden alarm. 'And it's not in very good taste either.'

'I have never been more serious,' he denied. 'I sensed that you would not welcome a sexual interest and I was prepared to get to know you as a friend instead.'

She felt a sudden surge of gratitude towards him. 'Thanks for being so nice,' she said, leaning over and giving him an impulsive hug.

Charles smiled ironically.

'I would not consider myself nice,' he chided. 'But I am your friend, Hyacinth.'

She saw Perlene in the library the following day, resolved on a sudden impulse to confide in her. She had not slept the previous night, too afraid of dreams and shadows even to turn the light out. Perlene, as usual, was in the centre of a crowd holding forth on one of her pet topics. Hyacinth wished she had that sort of confidence. She stood hesitantly at the edge, feeling at the periphery of all the excitement. She envied the Jamaica-raised students. She would have liked to be asked her opinion too. She knew as much about 'back home' as the others, but she was mindful of the fact that no one believed a word she said.

By the time Perlene caught sight of her she was feeling less like confiding in her, but the other girl waved with her usual impulsive vigour, and dived after her through the crowd.

'How long you been standing there? Why you never call me?' she asked breathlessly, threading her arm through Hyacinth's and marching her off.

'I didn't want to disturb you,' Hyacinth responded awkwardly.

'It wouldn't have mattered,' Perlene grinned, shrugging her shoulders dismissively. 'But how you been? I haven't seen you for weeks, girl, though I did glimpse you with Charles once or twice. How's the romance by the way?'

'Charles and I don't have a romance going,' Hyacinth said, reprovingly.

Perlene shrugged it off with a grin. 'You telling me you two so close and don't have romance? Hyacinth, sometimes I don't know what to do with you.'

Hyacinth ducked her head. 'I suppose I'm not ready for involvement,' she said, apologetically. She had often heard other students using that excuse and thought it sounded good.

'You know,' Perlene said, as they emerged into the warm October sunshine, 'I wonder if there's not something bad why you don't like men? Something that happen to you.'

Fear clutched at her. 'I don't think I could get involved with a non-Jamaican,' she said hastily, reasoning that it was not exactly a lie.

Perlene looked thoughtful, as if choosing her words carefully. She always did that now and Hyacinth felt hurt, knowing how open and spontaneous she was with the other black students. She was so full of life, always at the front of every new issue and debate, and Hyacinth often marvelled at how much she had learnt about the black community in the few years she had been in England. 'Hyacinth, don't you think it would be better to know a man for what he is rather than where he come from?' Perlene asked guardedly.

'It's a bit pointless if he comes from a different place,' Hyacinth said lamely.

'You are the same people,' Perlene persisted, making her flinch. It was so much like the words Charles had used.

'I am going back to Jamaica,' she said stubbornly.

'I wish you would listen to me about Jamaica,' Perlene sighed. 'Hyacinth, I really love Jamaica, but being blind to its faults is no way to show that love.'

'And what about loyalty?' Hyacinth was stung to retort. 'What about your country's good name?'

'I don't have no loyalty to what you thinking about. For me Jamaica is people. No amount of loyalty to the false independence the British left will provide jobs and fill hungry bellies.'

'Let's not get into that again,' Hyacinth cut in, feeling sudden impatience. She and Perlene could never agree. The other girl just couldn't understand that people had to make sacrifices, that not everyone in a poor country could be well-off.

Perlene grinned impulsively. 'Let's go get some coffee and I'll bore you with the letter I got from Mama,' she said suddenly.

The urge to confide in someone receded as exam considerations came to the fore. Hyacinth saw little of Perlene and Charles now, spending most of her time either in the library or the lab. She knew her work was good; her tutor told her that they expected her to get at least an upper second. The offer of a postgraduate place at the university in Jamaica further bolstered her, and even the tensions of the chemistry finals were handled with quiet confidence.

It was afterwards, in the idle time between exams and results, that Charles invited her to dinner again. She had accepted, knowing Perlene would be there, and had been a little put out when the other had not shown. 'She had to go to a meeting,' Charles said apologetically. 'I left a message in your pigeon-hole, but I see you did not get it.' She had pretended it was all right, but what she really needed was Perlene's light-hearted humour, not Charles' seriousness. The waiting for results seemed endless, the certainty before the exams replaced by the old inadequacies and doubts. Tonight she felt tense and edgy, and she knew that he must see it.

'Do you feel uneasy, being alone with me like this?' Charles asked as they sat in awkward silence after the meal.

'Gracious, no,' she said guiltily, having been thinking of ways to excuse herself without being rude. 'Why should I, anyway?'

'Because of the last time we were alone together in this flat.'

Hyacinth stiffened. 'That's a long time ago,' she said, in a strained voice.

Charles shook his head. 'There is so much pain inside of you. Don't hide away, please, Hyacinth,' he said gently.

She felt sick. Supposing he suspected what had happened? Her mind scrambled around, looking for a way to throw him off.

'Is it sex you fear?' he persisted.

'Of course not!' she said too quickly.

'Do you trust me?' Charles asked suddenly.

Hyacinth nodded warily, not sure of his direction. She was certainly not afraid of Charles. What she feared was what his persistence might unearth.

'Are you against sex before marriage?' he asked now.

It was on her tongue to say she was against it full stop, but she restrained herself, shaking her head instead.

'Would you do it?' he asked now, watching her carefully, adding when she did not answer, 'I think whatever is wrong is connected with sex, and maybe partaking of it would be the way to exorcise such a ghost.'

Hyacinth's fingers curled into her palms. Sex with Charles? Somehow it didn't seem such a bad idea. Supposing she could get rid of the nightmare? Wouldn't it be worth the chance?

'Do you mean sleep with you?' she asked, playing for time.

'Yes,' he said bluntly. 'I feel we have grown very close, and I think it is not self-flattery to say that you trust me.'

He was right, of course, she did trust him. Maybe she could get rid of the burden of guilt that weighed her down. If sleeping with a man would help, why not? Why not Charles, who was harmless, whom she trusted?

He had not told her it would be such a painful, messy business, she thought to herself as she lay there, staring dry-eyed at the ceiling after the fumbling, the slipping and the pain had stopped. She felt sick disgust, her mind an incoherent jumble full of anger and self-loathing. One sentence had whirled round with clarity, on and on since the pain and revulsion started: 'Incest flourished where the roads were bad.'

'Are you OK?' His voice seemed to come from afar, and she hated him for what he had done, for the false concern that had led her into his trap. She turned her head away. He was just like her father . . . no, worse. He had turned that lump into a hateful, painful reality. She had to concentrate, force her mind from the hysteria that threatened to overwhelm her. She had to move.

Then she was stumbling off the bed, fumbling for her clothes. She had to get away from that smell, so much like her father's pants, and wash the horror from between her legs. She felt soiled, sickness bubbling up in her throat with seething insistence.

'Hyacinth, what is the matter?'

She couldn't talk to him now, she had to hide the shame of her nakedness and go. Her fingers fumbled as she hauled on her sweatshirt, stuffed her bra in her jeans pocket in her haste.

'I'm sorry. I did not realise you were a virgin, and I have little experience with that.'

Where were her shoes? Oh God! she thought in panic, can't he see he's making me sick?

'You should have told me. I did not know I was causing you such anxiety.'

Why didn't he just shut up? Where were her shoes? She was going to scream if he did not shut up soon. Her shoes! Thank God! Christ, the tongue was bent in, she had to take it off again. She wouldn't be sick here, had to get out. The salt water was bubbling in her mouth and she breathed deeply. If only she had a polo mint. She had to keep breathing — in, out, in, out — just like they taught her at school; like she had done in the house of her father. She hardly noticed the tears streaming down her face, catching in the corner of her mouth. She had to get back. Had to wash the slime and dirt out of herself.

'Hyacinth, please, we have to talk!'

But she was out of the door, groping down the stairs. Now she could take great gulps of air, flush the horrible smell from her lungs. But in her mind, the nightmare thing still wriggled inside her, painful and sickening. She had to get back to campus, wash away the filth. She would be safe in her little room.

'River to the bank Cobalik?'

'One deh deh Cobalik, tek it put it down the alley.'

Hyacinth concentrated hard, listening to the sound of stones knocking on the ground, ears straining to pick up clues from the giggles and the whispers. She had guessed six right, six whole turns, she had never got six before.

'River to the bank Cobalik?'

'None noh deh deh Cobalik, a fool you a fool me Cobalik, a lie you a tell me . . .'

God, she wanted to go to the toilet bad. She was jiggling from foot to foot, wanting to stay, needing to go.

'River to the bank Cobalik?'

She had to go, but she just couldn't miss her turn.

'None noh deh deh Cobalik . . .'

It hurt down between her legs, a burning, aching pain that was in her head as well. She had to go. Had to go now. Then she was running, the burning worse as she moved. She dashed through the pretty white gate, brushing past Aunt Joyce, hardly hearing her anger. She thought she would never make it, but finally she was sitting there, leaning back with relief as it gushed out. She tried to force the flow, had to get back before they moved on without her. She was straining but all she could feel was the wetness rising around her bottom, filling up the toilet bowl, and she stopped in alarm as it trickled down her legs and splashed on the nice pink carpet. At last it began to ease, a never-ending trickle replacing the slowing gush. She would keep this last bit in, she just could not afford to lose her turn.

The sun was bright in her eyes, but why was the air so damp? She could see the game going on in the distance, the ringworm boy was Cobalik now. He was standing against her tree, straining his ears while they moved about behind him. Disappointment stabbed her. It was her turn, she was Cobalik, they had no right to move on without her. Anger made her heart race. She wanted to tear at him, drag him out of the way. If only she had the courage to tell him. If only he was not so big and evil. Even from where she was standing she could see the lump, mocking and threatening her, daring her to object. God, she wanted the toilet again. Hyacinth stood by the gate, the need to go again warring with the need to fight to get her turn. She hesitated, feet vibrating with the desire to move forward. But finally she turned away, defeat slumping her shoulders. No one would help her any more and she could never face him on her own. If he hurt her like he did before, none of them would care. Tears formed at the back of her eyes, disappointment moving inside her like a sad, dark thing.

Then she was lying in her bed, fully clothed, the light shining in her eyes. 'God, I must be sweating,' she thought, feeling the dampness all around. One hand moved, encountered soggy wetness, recoiled in horror. There was damp irritation against her lower back, a slippery acidness between her legs that mingled with the dull persistent ache. 'I wet the bed,' she whispered in shame and disgust. 'Big woman like me and I wet the bed.' The sickness moved about inside her, and she felt too disheartened to move. She turned her gaze away from the light, her eyes smarting as the slow tears slipped out.

The next day Charles came to see her, and Hyacinth crouched behind the door, her heart beating rapidly, a cornered animal, sure he would find a way in. He knocked and rattled the door, calling out to her, and she cowered, burying her head in her hands praying he would leave. She was frightened to leave the room after he had gone, and only ventured out when she had no choice, always watching out for him. She felt they were all watching her, that all the students knew what had happened to her. She did not even dare see Perlene, sure that Charles had told her, that her guilt was plain to see. Only the thought of Jamaica sustained her. The results will soon be out and I'll go to Aunt Joyce, she told herself with determination. Yet when they came, she was too afraid of him to check, ringing up the school secretary and asking her instead. Even the knowledge that her scholarship to Jamaica was now secure offered her little joy.

The day before she was due to leave the campus, Perlene came to see her. This time she let her in, reasoning that, after the following day, their paths need never cross again.

'You are one hard woman to track down,' Perlene said, bursting through the door as soon as the key was turned. 'Charles and I been looking everywhere for you.'

Hyacinth stiffened, searched the other's face intently, sure that she must know.

'I haven't been around,' she answered evasively, eyes sliding away from the direct gaze.

'Pity. You missed the best party ever, we all went round to cheer Charles up as he was a bit down.' Hyacinth muttered something non-committal, fingers curling into tight fists as Perlene chatted on. 'I'm sure you are going to meet him before you go,' she said in compensation. There was a pause and Hyacinth shifted uncomfortably when the other girl started again. 'I don't suppose I'll see you again before you leave, and I have to go to Trinidad next week for a month. Anyway, I wrote down my address for you, in case you need somewhere. Mama and Papa already know about you and they want to meet you.'

'Thanks,' Hyacinth said gratefully, accepting the paper the other girl had thrust into her hand.

'I only wish I could have done more,' Perlene said dryly. They stood looking at each other in the sudden awkward silence goodbyes always bring, and Hyacinth felt the tears start in her eyes. Perlene suddenly moved, threw her arms around Hyacinth, hugging her impulsively. Hyacinth responded to the unexpected warmth, felt the burning heat as tears began to spill.

'Don't be such a dodo,' Perlene said, stepping back, her face also wet. 'I'll see you in Jamaica, you dummy, and we can pick up the thread from there.'

Hyacinth smiled back, wiping her eyes with an impatient gesture. 'I'll miss you,' she said softly.

Perlene blinked, then walked to the door, regaining much of her composure. 'Take care of yourself, Hyacinth. And don't get hurt too badly.' With that cryptic statement, she slipped through the door. Hyacinth wondered what she had meant by it. Still, it was comforting to know that someone cared. She pushed the thought away almost as soon as it had come. Perlene was not the only one who cared. Her aunt was there. Florence and Cynthia as well. She would be happy again soon. All the sordid evil she had found in England would return to the realm of her nightmares, where they should have stayed.

Ten

'A can tek you as far as Tower Hill, and you gwine haffe pay me first.'

Hyacinth looked around blankly at the unfamiliar landscape. 'But I have to go further than that, you knew that when you drove me here,' she said, a desperate edge in her voice.

'That true, yes,' the man agreed readily, scratching his head under the thin cap he wore. 'But if a tek you it gwine cost more. It noh safe fa rich foreign lady, but it noh safe fa taxi cab neither, and nat even bus will run deh.'

She wanted to tell him to turn back, sick apprehension building inside her. What if someone attacked her? She had seen taxis on Lumber Street, why didn't they run past Tower Hill? She shifted restlessly, dislodging one of the parcels balanced on the seat beside her. The sound it made drew her attention, causing an attack of conscience. She had been in Jamaica over a week, and had not even visited her aunt or her friends. She could see the driver watching her, waiting impatiently for her to make up her mind, and she reached for her bag with resignation.

The car bumped along after that, sometimes slowing almost to a stop. The motion made her feel sick and she wondered how such places could exist in a modern city like Kingston. Her stomach turned, the dirt making her shake her head in horror and dismay. As the car pulled up outside a tangled mess of shacks, a group of surly-looking men started to gather, looking hostile and threatening. Hyacinth's whole body recoiled, nerves screaming against the stupidity of leaving the safety of the taxi.

'Dat is it,' the driver said, when she made no move to leave the car. 'You sure is the right place?'

Hyacinth nodded reluctantly, eyes sliding with horror over the squalor, mouth dry with anticipation as she fumbled with the door handle.

'You want me to wait?' the driver asked.

'Yes please,' she said hastily, the man suddenly seeming civilised and friendly, in spite of all the silent criticisms she had heaped on his head during the drive. He was safe, a part of her clean ordered world. What was she doing back here? How could she be here, after she had vowed it would not happen? Why must she always come back to so much dirt? She had to get a grip of herself, had to remember she was just visiting.

She would have liked to deny that she was in the right place, but the familiarity of weathered wood and corroded zinc refused to be dismissed. Her breakfast churned alarmingly inside her stomach, the bumpy ride and the shock pouring the salt of sickness into her mouth. The smell was like a physical blow, dredging up smells and tastes from long, half-buried memories; and she did not know whether heat or fear caused the sweat to trickle between her shoulder blades. Her hands gripped the parcels like a lifeline as she squeezed past the men who deliberately blocked the alleyway, feeling the hands, the jumbled sound of ribald comments ringing in her ears. She wanted to run as she reached the other side, terror hammering at her, screaming at her to get away. She could hear them behind her, voices laced with menace and intent.

'Incest flourished where the roads were bad.'

The sentence frightened her, popping into her head unexpectedly, along with the memory of her father and his obscene lump. She prayed that they wouldn't follow her, that she would not get killed. Her feet faltered as she saw another crowd of them clustered round the doorway of a record shack. She mustn't let them see how frightened she was. Taking deep breaths, she pushed the horror away, kept it at the back of her mind. Hate and suspicion radiated from the crowd as they caught sight of her, and there was a surliness about the way they lounged about, staring insolently as she passed.

This was not the place she remembered. Why had she not listened to Perlene? Or at least written to her aunt? Aunt Joyce would have told her how things were, would never have let her come down this road. Now she was forced to continue walking, too frightened to turn back, knowing what waited in that direction. She could never remember a path so long, so choked with dust and rubbish. Every time the wind stirred a piece of faded newspaper, or rustled one of the dry pathetic bushes, she would tense. Her whole body shook, the shivers starting deep inside and spreading everywhere.

'I'm such a fool,' she repeated over and over again, trying to gain some comfort from the admission. The hotel had warned her. Perlene had begged her. It was like Lumber Street all over again. She had seen it on the news in England. The streets of Kingston at night, lit up by fire and the blaze of guns. But even Lumber Street seemed cheerful now. At least the silence was broken by the constant noise of traffic horns and the sound of rasta greetings.

She came across it suddenly. The clammy cherry trees were still there, twin sentinels, their red and white cherries glinting in the sun. She knew that behind them was the gully, its crumbling slopes a raw wound in the ground. Her mind screamed rejection of the wooden shack, refused the ragged familiarity of the splintered door. She stood hesitant, disappointment a physical blow. It will be better inside, she told herself stoutly, clutching her parcels closer still. She was painfully aware of the eyes peering from the other shacks, the hostility all around her, shapes circling sus-piciously, out of sight, yet glimpsed out of the corner of her eye.

She thought longingly of the taxi, the hotel, England, all so far away and safe. God, how civilised England seemed now. Steeling herself, she walked up to the shack, climbed the two unsteady stairs with weak and shaky legs. She gritted her teeth with determination, forcing her hand to knock. Maybe Aunt Joyce will walk me to the taxi, she thought hopefully. Maybe she doesn't even live here. Maybe she didn't know where to find me when she moved. The thought was comforting, giving her strength to push the door open when no reply came. The smell made her recoil, sickened her as it penetrated her nose, entered her mouth, lingered and was swallowed. Her stomach felt tender from fear and abuse, and she wished she had not eaten breakfast. She stood there, blinded by the sun and the shuttered windows, while shock moved through her in continuous waves.

If the outside was familiar, the inside was not. And yet it tugged the memory. She could not remember living in this hovel, could not recall this decay and neglect. Yet hadn't she done those faded childish drawings pinned on the wall? Wasn't that dust-covered table her aunt's pride and joy, the one that you could see your face in after it was polished on Saturdays? Then there was the worn armchair, the now greasy crucifix and the picture of the Last Supper on the wall. The nightmare place set the memories off; her aunt's bulk wedged in the chair, drying the comb, waiting for her to come, hair wet from a recent wash. She and Florence sitting on the wooden floor colouring pictures, Cynthia burning . . . She snatched her mind back from that one, pushed the orange flames away. Where was Aunt Joyce? What had happened to her? She would never have allowed the pile of rubbish in the corner, the dust, the smell.

'Is who dat dere?'

Hyacinth jumped, heart racing with a sudden surge of hope. The thin reedy voice coming from the curtained doorway was definitely not Aunt Joyce's.

'Anybady deh deh?'

She wondered if the woman would help her, could tell her where her aunt was. No harm in trying, she thought bracingly, stepping over a pile of bottles and picking her way across the dimly lit floor.

Clutching her parcels firmly, she edged round the curtain, gagging at the concentration of smell in the airless room. It was like a mingling of dirt, drink and urine and it teased out her own shame, still a wide and bleeding wound.

The double bed she had shared with her aunt was gone, in its place a broken-down single one. On it lay a withered old woman, covered with a torn and grimy sheet. Hyacinth looked away from the lined, drawn face, with its sunken eyes and air of death. She felt disgust at the discarded items of clothing littering the place, the bottles piled untidily to one side of the bed.

'I'm looking for Miss Joyce Williams,' she said, voice strained.

There was a gasp from the bed and the woman struggled to sit up, bringing the smell of stale rum and terminal sickness closer. Hyacinth's eyes watered with the increased discomfort of her stomach, and she stepped back in alarm when the woman stretched out shaky hands to her, tensing herself for the begging words.

'Lord be praised,' the thin voice creaked out. 'Is Hyacinth come back fram England! Hyacinth noh faget me. Come chile, come mek me look pan yu.'

Hyacinth stared at her in horror, frozen with shock and disbelief, her mind struggling to reject what she had heard. The bony body shifted uncertainly on the bed, feet moving with painful deliberation, looking thin and pathetic as they braced feebly to take the fragile weight of the emaciated body. Then it was standing, swaying uncertainly, movement unsure as it started towards her. The mouth opened in a grimace of a smile, showing gaps in the discoloured teeth, gold glinting just where her aunt's gold tooth had been. She stood frozen, head shaking in denial as the nightmare came to life. Her mind screamed rejection, body bathed in cold sweat, as she trembled and whimpered, unable to bear what she could see.

The thud of the parcels falling from her nerveless fingers brought life back to her frozen limbs and she stumbled backwards, eyes glued on the bony thing.

'There is no harm in it so long as I know the reality,' Charles' voice said from across the months. This is not reality, her mind rejected. The reality is not here, this is the nightmare. She crashed through the other room, stumbling over a pile of bottles, hand skidding on the table to save herself, recoiling from the grease on it. And then she was in the sunshine, dragging deep gulps of warm air into her lungs, heart hammering, stomach churning madly.

'Hyacinth Williams? Noh Hyacinth?'

The sound of her name brought a fresh wave of trembling, and she prayed nothing else would happen before she woke up. It had to be a dream, just could not be real. Now she tensed as a woman, shapeless sagging body in a washed-out grey dress and worn leather sandals, walked towards her. She wanted to run, to get away before she found out any more. She didn't even wonder how the other knew her name. The horror she had just left seemed to drain her, leaving her unable to move, and she stood almost docile, looking blankly at the woman, her mind the only thing alive and in revolt.

'A suppose you ca'an memba me,' the woman said, voice full of bitter irony, 'but I memba yu. Aside from de press hair and de clothes yu noh change.'

Hyacinth shifted uncomfortably. 'You remember me?' she asked hesitantly, fearfully.

The woman's hair, her face, looked grey and neglected, reminding her uncomfortably of the days in her father's house. The other smiled, warmth seeping into the hard brown eyes. 'We use to tief pepper dung Cassava Piece, you, me and Cynthia before she did get dead in de fire.'

Hyacinth felt a fresh wave of shock. This was Florence! Cynthia was dead! Where were the children of her dream? She swallowed painfully, refusing to think of Lumber Street.

'I can't remember you,' she said stubbornly, refusing to let the dream world slip away. She thought of the elegant stockings and silk scarves she had brought with despair. What would such a woman know of such things? And Cynthia, she had brought a present for her too, how could her mind have played such a cruel trick on her? Guilt and sadness weighed her down. She could not bear it, could not remain standing there in the heat and fly-filled poverty. She had to get away, back to where she could be alone, could recover from the horror of this day.

'How come yu goh a England an noh even write dawg to your auntie?' the woman asked accusingly, as she made to turn away. 'Yu aunt did grow yu fram yu bawn, treat yu like fe him own. How yu do it Hyacinth?' Hyacinth shifted uncomfortably, she had to get away from this place. The bile was rising inside her, bitter in her mouth.

'I didn't know,' she pleaded wretchedly, wondering if the woman would attack her. She looked so big and aggressive, standing feet apart, arms resting on her broad hips. 'I had a lot of problems,' Hyacinth added, feeling a desperate need to convince the other.

The woman looked at her in disbelief. 'Is years yu auntie sick now,' she said shaking her head, 'an is you mek it, an yu neva even sen somting fe pay docta bill.'

The injustice of it moved through her, causing a dull anger to rise inside her. 'She was not sick when I left for England,' she pointed out stiffly, 'and anyway she seems more drunk than sick to me.'

'Is when yu neva rite that she start drink de wite rum,' the other returned, glaring at her with hostility.

Hyacinth felt tongue-tied, bewildered. What more could she say to this bitter, hostile woman?

'Well, now yu deh ya, a wa yu gwine do?' the other persisted, pressing aggressively forward to glare at her.

'I? . . . Well, nothing,' she said, stumbling over the words, not quite knowing what the woman meant.

'Doctas cost money,' came the angry retort. 'Is me one look afta yu auntie and me haffe look bout man an pickney to.'

Contempt seeped back into Hyacinth. She was on familiar ground now. This woman was no different from the rest, all she wanted was money. Well, if that's what she wanted, she could have it. At least it would shut her up. Rooting about in her bag, she extracted her purse, took out two dollars, offered them, watching the other all the time. The woman had been watching her with scorn, and now she looked her up and down with contempt.

'A doan need money so bad a ca'an do widout dat!' she said, shaking her head, sorrow and anger mingling in her worn, tired face. 'No sah, Hyacinth,' she said heavily, the anger full of sad regret now. 'Yu is a different person wid yu speakey spokey ways. Yu noh belang ya soh.' She turned abruptly, walking away, still shaking her head, muttering to herself.

Hyacinth watched her walk away, the last words ringing in her ears. Guilt and rejection burned through her; while the shock of that dark and dirty room still caused half-formed images to buzz around her mind. She felt weary. Deep inside her bones and in her heart she knew the woman was right. But right now she did not care, all she wanted was to get away. She moved jerkily, about to turn away, when the woman's voice stopped her once again:

'Yu Auntie doan have long, an is bes she noh know what a dawg you tun. A tel yu dis as good advice Hyacinth, true we was fren one time. Go back whe yu come fram. We noh like fariginers ina J.A.'

Each word, like a knife wound, stabbed and ripped inside her. Where did they expect her to go? Why did everyone reject her? She wanted to shout that she was sorry, that the whole thing was just a horrible mistake. Maybe she would wake up now. Surely she should have done already?

'Go back whe you come fram.'

The words whirled about inside her head. How many times had she heard that since coming to Jamaica, or was it since she had gone to England? She felt rejected, unbelonging. Where was the acceptance she had dreamt about, the going home in triumph to a loving, indulgent aunt? Was this what she had suffered for? It was all so pointless, all for nothing. There was a wringing pain in her chest, and tension made her jaw ache as tears refused to fall from burning eyes. But inside she cried, pain-racked sobs that made breathing hard and walking a laboured thing. She wondered if they all noticed her pain, the people in the street glaring their hate, the curious taxi-driver. She felt exposed, her blackness ugly and rejected even among her own kind.

Hyacinth did not remember quite how she got back to the large hotel room, its impersonal air exactly what she needed. She still felt dazed and her head ached from too much horror and the sun. She remembered England as a child, the beatings, the jeers. 'Go back where you belong,' they had said, and then she had thought she knew where that was. But if it was not Jamaica, where did she belong?

The woman who had been Florence flashed before her, body shapeless from childbearing, face lined with suffering. She shuddered at the thought that she might have been that woman, pushed it aside, remembered instead the carefree girl, her friend. Her mind drifted back to Lumber Street, the house on the corner where Cynthia had lived. Cynthia always better off than the two of them. Always unhappy because her father beat her. Her father who, they had whispered, was mad. She could feel the heat on her back again as she remembered that night. The man going mad, she and Florence running, the heavy door slamming, and Cynthia clawing at the window, burning.

Laughter drifted under her door as footsteps passed by and she envied the other guests. The tourists who came for sun, sea, excitement. They all had a place to go to, they were not forced to stay as she was. She could not dine with them tonight, stomach still full of the sight and smells, the fetid heat of that awful poverty. She felt a stab of irritation as more guests passed her door. How could they come here, live like lords and ladies? What justice said that to be black was to be inferior? It was so unfair, her mind cried out in frustration. She had run back to where black people ruled, only to find that it was all a dream. They were all still slaves, still poor, still trodden down.

She thought longingly about Perlene. She would be in Trinidad now. Why had she not listened to the other girl? Perlene knew. She belonged. She remembered the other girl's address still safely in her bag. 'I'll go and see her parents,' she thought wistfully. 'Maybe they will accept me.' But even as she thought it, she rejected the idea, the day's rejections still too fresh to court another one. Her mind spun back to that lined and bitter woman, moved on to the withered thing that had proved to be her aunt. It went round and round from one to the other, a circular thought. And always, behind it all, her father waited, crouching in the shadows, beating at her with all the horrors she had faced, laughing and mocking all her attempts at escape. And inside her, deep down, buried inside her woman's body, trapped and bleeding in the deepest recesses of her, a young girl screamed. As the scream echoed in her mind, the tears seeped out and Hyacinth knew she would never be free until that child had healed.

The three of them were in their secret place again and the sound of their voices mingled with the busy sound of movement and activity all around them. It was safe in the little green cave, the recesses of the bushes laden with long-stemmed hibiscus and yellow trumpet-flowers, buzzing with insect activities. She could hear the whine of the doctor bird's beating wings coming faintly through the thicket. The warm afternoon air folded comfortingly around her shoulders, tried to drive away the pain and sadness that ached at the back of her mind. She could hear the weak sick voice calling out to her, pleading for help, bitter anger and hostility in the other one. She heard the screams, the desperation of the thin, weak voice, and felt powerless to help. So she sat there, full of guilt and horror, not knowing what to do. It was safe there, in the little green cave. Safe and lonely and sad. But was there anything out there but rejection and all the uncertainty she had hidden from? Safe inside her cave, Hyacinth lay back in the sweet-smelling grass and cried.